Throughout Andrew's life, as early as he can remember, he has always had a creative and wild imagination, but one terror inducing nightmare that always remains close to the surface of both his conscious and subconscious, is that of the undead, Zombies or "The Walking Dead" they since he can remember have both fascinated and terrified him, the reason being, that they are the pure manifestation of our own self destructive nature boiled down to its purest and primal form, and have the capability to be our slate wiper, our extinction event, add them into an apocalyptic survival situation, and the scenarios are infinite, and within Dead Plague he has written a few scenarios that, shows through his eyes how such an event can affect each and every one of us.

Andrew Tomlinson

Dead Plague

AUSTIN MACAULEY PUBLISHERS™

LONDON · CAMBRIDGE · NEW YORK · SHARJAH

A CIP catalogue record for this title is available from the British Library.

ISBN 9781528937115 (Paperback)
ISBN 9781528937207 (Hardback)
ISBN 9781528941143 (Audiobook)
ISBN 9781398402836 (ePub e-book)

www.austinmacauley.com

First Published 2023
Austin Macauley Publishers Ltd®
1 Canada Square
Canary Wharf
London
E14 5AA

Dead Plague is a collection of short stories set in a post-apocalyptic pandemic, where an unknown viral plague has ravaged mankind to near extinction as it reanimated the dead and their only insistence is to seek the flesh of the living, and will not cease their relentless hunger driven search until all sentient life is cleansed, leaving not but the fauna to reclaim the earth, the survivors face not only the dead but the living as small communities become increasingly desperate, all essence of civilisation is stripped away and the notion of kill or be killed becomes the damned mantra of the dead world.

Each story is relatively connected, in the fact that the survivors have to battle against the dead or the remnants of humanity to survive, trying to seek salvation, redemption, hope in an otherwise dead world, these are not set in any chronological order.

Hope

Four specialised military brothers seek out revenge after a scavenging party of theirs is ambushed by marauders, a small band of despicable almost inhuman people, that raid, and pillage surviving settlements to survive and in doing so their wages for their vile work is execution, the brothers are elite and are deemed saviours to the people, they set up a fortified base known to others as the sanctuary, where all who are trying to re-assemble what life was like before are welcome, they are the new forged hope that keeps the people alive.

Loss

A father coming to terms with his mortality, after being bitten now must confront his worst fear, saying goodbye to his daughter, the physical pain from the virus slowly killing his body is nothing compared to the emotional turmoil in knowing he will be leaving the one thing that he holds dear behind.

Pathogen

A haematologist is on call, when on the night shift an incident occurs and police and medical staff are scrambled, brought in from an attack, two dead and three wounded, while proceeding with the standard medical procedures for suspected rabies attack, the haematologist makes an historic discovery but one that will undoubtedly end humanity, an unknown living bacterium that awakens the dead sending them into a feeding frenzy, that is transferred via physical contact, a new strain of pathogen.

Forever

Even within a world where it seems the nightmares have broken free and the demons have escaped hell, that something as pure as love can still be kindled, two friends make their way to a secluded location, unsure of the future, while one hides a secret, pondering the hidden love she holds for her best friend, and petrified of what would happen if she confesses her long sheltered emotion, that is if a huge horde of the dead doesn't get to them first.

Survival

Humans with no restraint are nothing but monsters, in order to survive they take to setting ambushes for unsuspecting wanders looking for a haven away from death, but sometimes the predators fall prey, in this case a couple now separated, one being injured seeks shelter and medical aid within an abandoned hospital, she must treat her wounds before infection sets in, then find her partner, all while avoiding the dead that inhabit the surrounding area, in these times she must do what she must to survive.

Dead

A man devoid of all emotion but anger finds himself turning into the reaper, to remove the damned souls that prey on the weak and innocent, his mission is to remove these human shit stains, in a single night of glorious blood lust, however after his mission is completed, he makes a startling realisation.

Hope

The day hell spewed out its inhabitants upon the earth they came with a savage relentless hunger, and they sort to ease that hollow ache by devouring human flesh.

Within a year the global population was desolated, the remaining military factions of combined countries decided it was strategically sound to now wield their nuclear weapons and lay waste to cities and countries in hope of eradicating the dead plague but to no avail; the decaying world belongs to the hell bound creatures, it has now become a waiting game to see how long it takes for the denizens of hell to starve and return to the black abyss from which they crawled out.

The days are shorter and darker, the nights longer and colder, crueller winter is upon us and her cruel frozen hands grasp hold of everything she rests her vicious eyes on, the reality that nature is reclaiming her planet with a restless rage is ever present, she aims to rid the remaining parasites off of her the same ones that were once ignorantly killing her.

But this day the cold is not the problem, this day we do not fight the freezing bitterness of the ice; this day we seek the warm blood of our enemies, the inhuman ones that would take pleasure in destroying our new forged hope.

The dark shadow of my enemy, I see him through the white veil, the snow drives down hard, I see him as we approach 10 meters directly in front of me.

'Contact ahead,' I whisper as I press the contact buttons on my throat mic.

We approach from his rear silently ghost like.

In 5 meters the others take a knee covering all angles as I continue my approach, I sling my weapon and creep forward, he stands shivering in the cold, a sentry, I hear the clattering of his teeth, I slowly move up and begin to wrap my hands around the back of his head following under the jaw line being careful not to make contact, he doesn't notice anything, my hands are mid neck, I act with trained ferocity; my left hand covers his mouth and nose as my right arm snakes round his throat. To the crook of my left arm there I jam in my right hand and squeeze shut his trachea as his brain and body is deprived of oxygen; he weakens, his body weight slumps into me, I hold him up, I slowly asphyxiate him to death, he is the first.

I pinch the contact buttons on my throat mic even though we are only spread 6 meters apart; the ever-constant blizzard makes it hard to hear.

'3, 4 flank left rally at the rear.'

They move off fading into the falling white; myself and 1 move off flanking right.

1 has point, I cover the rear.

Covertly 1 eliminates another contact using the same stealth technique that I used.

He leaves the corpse where it lays as I did and as the others will do the climate is on our side for once she will unwillingly aid us and conceal our presence.

Under normal circumstances we would never set on any other survivors with or without cause, but these are not survivors these are creatures black souled steeped in the blood of innocence, they raid our convoys, murder, torture, rape women and devour men and children this has happened in the past but it will not happen in the future. The dread beings that take to dealing with the devil selling their souls for a twisted existence they delve in the disposable pleasures of day to day life not concerning themselves with meaningful pursuits, we on the other hand covet the meaningful pursuits the pursuit of reclaiming our lives, the pursuit of not having to live in fear, not having to live in squaller, to remove the dead plague that craves the living flesh, the pursuit of lighting up the dark.

But today the dark prevailed and we aim to stub it out, this day they plotted, maimed, killed families, friends, brothers, daughters, sisters and sons and worse they have taken some of our own, some of the very people I swore that I would keep safe, I cannot abandon them to the will of demons, I will not.

Their compound is what was once a radio communications centre high in the peaks surrounded by trees. Situated in a clearing, snow drifts settle high and suffocate the rusting radio building and antenna, fractured satellite dishes and dead electrical cables are strewn about, the compound itself is situated below the ground approximately two levels; this was to ensure that the people given charge of the compound lived comfortably away from the biting cold, black smoke plumes from within through the roof and some light dimly glows from holes and fractured glass.

We RV (rendezvous) at the rear entrance, directly ahead two ghostly figures appear out of the white they cleared the left flank with ease and now proceed to stack up on our position.

We cover the area I nod to 3; he moves to me and begins to pick the lock after checking that the door is in-fact locked, I remain knelt covering my brother as the others cover me.

After a moment 3 gestures that the door is unlocked, he moves back right readying his weapon. I move right next to him in a shielding manner, 1 holds left and 4 covers rear right, I gently begin to turn the handle, with no sound the handle unlatches I bring my silenced Beretta M9 semiautomatic pistol up holding the easy loaded weight in my right hand; then cradling the bottom of the curved grip with my left after taking it off the cold handle, improving its accuracy, it's a double action 9x19mm Parabellum 15 round staggered box magazine fed side arm.

We each have one. I have mine ready as does 3, 1 readies his MP5SD3 Suppressed 9x19 small arms weapon with an integrated suppressor, a retractable butt-stock and red dot optic sight, it's a nice covert sub machine gun, with an effective firing range of 100 meters (328 feet), a fire rate of 800 rounds per minute, we each have this weapon with 4x30 round magazines and attached tactical torch with the exception of myself having an added fore grip and 1 having an ITL MARS combination red dot laser multi-purpose aiming reflex sight, 3 and 1 have an extra weapon; an impressive L74A1 pump action shotgun it's a Remington model 870 bottom loaded side ejecting; it's a 12 gauge 7 round fed system with an added cartridge in the breach

It's a brilliant weapon for going overt and with the spread of the shot prefect for the narrow corridors of the compound they each hold a full 40 shell cartridge belt.

After a moments ease I nod my head and push open the door. 1, myself and 3 immediately see the two sentries on guard duty, they are caught by surprise as the door flies open. The blistering cold drives inwards aiding us as the cold bites at their vision; we give them no quarter, no chance for alarm. We barrage 9mm pieces of silenced hellfire, they go down, I move inwards right hugging the wall; the instant stench of rusting metal infused with stale body odour fills my nostrils, 1 follows and hugs the left wall. We continue training our weapons down range as 3 and 4 join us.

I check the bodies for life, there is none.

'Clear.'

'3, 4 hold position.'

As I finish 3 holsters, his Beretta M9 unshoulders; his L74A1 Pump action, 4 takes up cover position down range and readies his suppressed MP5SD3, 3 takes up cover position from the door aiming down the corridor. He readies his 12 gauge.

1 continues to train down range, I look to him then to 4, he nods in reply then I look at 3 he looks back at me. He nods and I smile from the side of my mouth without parting my lips, I know my brother will be safe, he has done this many times but as my little brother I cannot help but fret as a big brother does as I do.

After a moment of emotional turmoil, I focus. I train my gaze down range to the unknown and silently proceed forward.

A dull metallic thud reverberates in the distance, we round the corner and come to a junction ahead; the corridor splits off ahead leading to rooms, then to the left rusting iron stairs eerily descend into the black bowls of the compound, I hand signal to 1 to proceed forward, he hesitates as to question my decision then proceeds in the designated direction, I peer down into the blackness where the ominous thud emanates. I remove my small LED tac light with my left hand, hold it forward and place my right hand over the top steadying my aim, I slowly step by step delve down disappearing into the darkness just as the natural light fades, I flick on my tac light a small beam illuminates the areas that I place it upon.

I hit the bottom no hostiles but a scent raises my danger awareness, cooking meat, I have smelled this exact same scent before; it is unlike any other but so distinct, it's as easily recognisable as any scent of flowers cooking human flesh, as the dead plague cover the earth devouring all life some survivors have taken to the unthinkable in desperation, I push forward down the corridor as it narrows, the metallic thud grows louder. I am close to the source, I shake away the flooding images of deduction of what the source of the sound could be, I need to be focused.

Before I reach the door, I flick off my tac light and place it back, then go for the door handle. The smell grows stronger now entwined with putrefaction and sweat, I flare my nostrils and heavily exhale through them to drive the stench out.

I grasp hold of the handle, it's warm, silently it opens. I found the source of the unsettling sound and find that my deductions were correct; the scene that my eyes witness would usually horrify me but I have seen dead corpses rise and ravenously rip, tear and devour living, screaming people, I do not let my compassion overcome me, I bury it, but I know that the scene is burnt deep into my sub-conscience and in my dreams I will relive the nightmare scenario.

Two men stand in the dim light to the far left; backs towards me they are hacking, chopping and butchering human cadavers. I move forward, weapon trained on the vile beings to the right, my movement is ghost like, they are none the wiser to my presence that is until I squeeze the trigger. A single hushed hiss of the weapon and the hard drop off the bastard as his lifeless corpse hits the floor. The second, puzzled by his companions action, before he can turn to face me I squeeze the trigger again and again two 9mm holes materialise in the side of the fiend's head, he drops too with a hard thud to the concrete, I place another round in my first victim's dome just to make sure. I then notice him, he lays upon the large thick blood-stained wooden table, both arms removed as well as his right leg, massive slices into his left where the femur joint attaches to the hip, the look of sheer terror still etched upon his face; eyes wide frozen in the last horrible moments of life, I know him. He was one of the medics captured, sorrow and guilt begin to come forward. I remove the emotions, it's hard to do so, they are so strong and fight me for control. I look around for further intel but instead hit the jackpot; the room is partly filled with canned goods, fuel and medical supplies; some that is ours but all of it is now ours.

I was about to face towards the source of the light; it's a large fire pit with two bodies skewered on rotisserie spikes held over the flames, the flesh sizzling as the fire and heat flick and lick upwards I notice the leftovers, piled bones and fouled organs. I clench my jaws tight; rage now begins to emanate from within. I allow it to surge, I will use it, mould it, training teaches us to do this as to un-wield the rage to let it swarm free throughout the core. It blinds and distorts the focus and judgement and that could lead to the death of my team, I inhale the rage and take hold of the reigns. I proceed forward through the opposite door and back up some more stairs. As I emerge I hear "friendly right" through my headset. Without looking 1 appears through the right-side door and joins me. I am holding at the near top of the steps.

'Sub-level clear.'

'Living quarters clear.'

'Prisoners located… alive and secure.'

I look to him and he looks back, he nods as I do in reply and we proceed forward. I hug the left wall, he hugs the right wall, we halt at the double doors of the main comms room. Before we enter the room; I holster my silenced beretta M9 and un-shoulder my suppressed MP5SD3. I hold it tight, the butt stock digging into my right shoulder I peer down the iron sight.

No thought, no time for that creep of doubt to set in, we act.

We kick open both doors as they fly open almost off the hinges. I see my first target, I squeeze the trigger; a flurry of 9mm projectiles spray out at 375 meters per second, my aim is true, each projectile sinks deep into my target's head and neck, he drops; unaware, the second target next to him, his reactions are not quick enough. As he recognises the threat, I squeeze and another flurry of hell fire bursts outwards, he's down, half left another, he brings his weapon up but his aiming is inaccurate. I drop on my right knee making myself smaller to hit, the rounds spray far right of me, mine, however connect spraying his torso. He twitches as the rounds bore through his soft skin and softer organs.

Our actions and might are swift, our justice true, none are left in our wake; for these are monsters, not men and they need to be put down.

'Left clear.'
'Right clear.'

We sweep throughout the room ensuring that it is in-fact clear; once we are sure I radio my men.

'3 and 4 compound cleared and secure, what's your SIT-REP (situation report) how copy?'

My radio goes silent for an instant then comes alive with 4's voice.

'Good, copy, all clear, we are all clear.'

'Roger that, hold position for bravo team's convoy, we will be escorting our surviving people out and gathering supplies, how copy?'

'4 copies all.'
'3 copies all.'

'Awesome work, lads.'

I radio through then I switch my comms over to another secure frequency.

'Bravo team convoy, this is alpha team, how copy?'

There's is a moment of silence then the radio crackles up again.

'Go for bravo team convoy.'

'Bravo team convoy, compound secured, you are clear to enter compound to retrieve six survivors and gather supplies how copy.'

'Bravo team copies en route.'

'Bravo team, switch to radio frequency 6 to maintain constant comms.'

'Roger that.'

I switch back to my main frequency and await response from bravo team.

The radio begins to speak.

'Alpha team, confirm radio frequency.'

'Bravo team, this is alpha team, radio frequency confirmed.'

Afterwards I switch radio frequency again to contact charlie team for a complete compound perimeter and to switch to frequency 6 as my brother joins my side, they do as requested, the radio goes silent, I place my left arm over my brother onto his shoulder in a slight embrace and we proceed to head towards the prisoner's holding cell.

I am part of a team of hell dawn worriers putting our own lives at risk to provide provisions and amenities to those we protect, friends, families, loved ones from the monsters that roam the devastated world beyond the gates of our sanctuary that we built from the ground up, we strive to maintain a substantial order of what the world once was to preserve humanity, to keep it alive so that when the time comes we can exhume the world from its decrepit crypt and return to times of peace and tranquillity, we strive to keep people alive, to not devolve into the beasts at our door and surrender our souls to the devil, our main objectives are to protect those who cannot protect themselves and to outlast the dreaded beings that now hunt all.

We are the watchful protectors; we are the hope that blooms and flourishes in people's hearts.

The blizzard has eased and now the large flakes of snow elegantly sway in the atmosphere, the cold is not as bitter, the wind chill has died, the day is somewhat of a success; out of the eight souls captured, we rescue six and gather much needed supplies, ammunition, weapons, canned goods, extra clothing, medical supplies, two generators and a good supply of fuel, four and a half barrels worth, we burn the departed and take our leave home.

The snow continues to glide and sway beautifully in the evening air, the sky is pure white, it melts harmoniously into the horizon, I admire the natural beauty of the snow, the pristine softness that blankets all.

'We have arrived.'

The faint crackle of the radio in the cab sparks to life, I ignore the conversation but my ears perk at the sound of the corpse focusing; I learn that there are approximately three wandering corpses tracking us, my interest is perked and I peer through the gaps in the reinforced siding to see in the distance shambling figures but there are more than 3, I briefly hope that the main gate is swiftly secured once we are let through, then my mind fades and wonders to higher peaked interests. Interests that lay in memories, particularly one in which I acquired not too long ago, it's still so intensely vivid, beautiful eyes and a perfect smile, I begin reminiscing the morning I awoke, the day I was assigned for the R-OP (rescue operation) how I was sweetly awoken by the warm rays of sun and gentle finger tips circling my chest, I remember my eyes opening and resting on a beautiful face, bright, blue eyes lovingly gazing back into mine, my chest seems to flutter madly with a warming sensation, it makes me smile, I drink in her image her magnificence, the perfect curl of her lashes, flawless white silky skin, the flush of blood in her cheeks as she blushes a tantalisingly warming colour, her perfectly pink inviting lips, waves of golden hair that glimmer and glow in the sun's rays, each long slithers of gold; a few stray strands gently curl down caressing her face, she beams an immensely glorious smile at me and I become entranced, I smile back and we gaze at each other, I ponder how such a perfect angel could fall for a mere man.

I recall brushing aside the rogue strands with my hand, her skin is warm, alive and so incredibly soft; her warmth flows into my hand as she embraces my caress, gently placing her fingertips on the back of my hand, I feel her touch. It invigorates me; my skin hairs stand on end; she closes her eyes and I await eagerly for her lashes to part so I may fall into them perfect eyes again.

She does and again as her eyes gaze fondly into mine, my heart flurries and flutters, warmth emanates from within such a feeling that I cannot place into words. I don't want it to end. I feel peace, harmony bliss… she is my love… she holds my heart… I have given it to her, and she has given hers to me.

She is my hope.

Loss

'TOURNIQUET! TOURNIQUET NOW!' I scream as I rip open the right trouser leg revealing the black hole of a wound, inside mid-thigh. As the material rips, it relaxes pressure from around it, and a thick jet of arterial blood spurts into the air past my face, I feel the warmth of the liquid and the smell of it, it splats on the inside of the truck.

'PRESSURE SQUEEZE!' Instantly four hands including my own pile on top of each other's with force trying to stop the un-natural flow of blood, it doesn't help that the guy we are trying to save is writhing, squirming about screaming, it's frustrating me.

'FUCKING TOURNIQUET NOW!' I scream above the screaming.

'HOLD HIM DOWN!'

He's moving too much; I feel the blood welling up in between my fingers and hands making them slippy as well as the others, if he doesn't stop we can't help and he's going to die.

My patience is waning as this guy continues to panic, scream and whimper, his actions are strengthened by the jumping and jutting of the moving truck.

'FUCK THIS!' I say as I remove my hands from his wound ball up my right fist and throw it with all the frustration and anger that I have right into the right side of his jaw, everyone hears the crack as his jaw almost wraps around his head, his eyes roll up into his skull and he falls limp with a thud, I instantly check his pulse, it's low and steady which means that the blood won't be pumping as fast escaping from the wound, I go straight back to his leg.

'Tourniquet,' I say with a low authoritative tone.

The back of the truck is silent and all six pairs of eyes are on me wide and in shock; one pair I notice strays away looking for the tourniquet, I place my hands down back on top of the others stemming the flow of blood from the wound, instantly I see another pair of hands begin to wrap a black nylon strap around the leg above our hands, below the hip; they velcro the strap down and then take hold of the tension stick. Beginning to twist the strap tightens cutting off the flow of blood to the wound.

'It's tight.'

A male voice states.

I slowly take my hands off away from the others, so far no welling up of blood no spurting, slowly another pair of hands remove, again no spurting and finally the last two, the results are satisfying, a little pooling, but no spurting or pumping, the tourniquet has done its job.

A sigh of relief is reverberated around within the back of the truck, the men begin arguing fecklessly amongst themselves, I couldn't really care at this point, I push myself back against the inside of the truck, I feel the vibrations in my back and into my chest, its calming, I see my breath plume out in front of me as I exhale, I slowly close my eyes, I feel my eye lashes entwine, I focus on my breathing, I focus on the cold air as I draw in breath; I focus on how the cold air dissipating into my chest, I focus on the intense stinging pain and the aching which follows, how it creeps up my leg like it has a mind of its own and aims for the vital parts of me.

I have been bitten on my left thigh, left hip, right forearm and right shoulder, the burning sensation converges and begins to travel to my brain, as the virus moves its slowly killing nerves which cry out in pain as they wither strangled, as I will do the same.

As I ponder my ill fate a sense of dread befalls me, I feel it in my heart, a dark heavy hanging sensation but it's not for my death, it's for my daughter and her fate, who will watch over her, protect her.

My mind races with turmoil and conflict, with so many bite wounds I don't have much time, and I can't tell anyone as they will put me down instantly, so I will conceal my condition until it is time to which I will take care of myself.

So, for now I discretely clean and bandage my wounds.

We arrive at our compound passing the first checkpoint and into the garage area, I give thanks to the decrease in pace, the last 10 minutes, every bump and ditch, every shudder of the truck, the vibrations that shook me, it felt as though my bones were shattering, by this time my breathing is heavy, I am sweating profusely and my temperature has risen, I exit the truck trying to look as normal as possible hiding the fact that every inch of me is screaming in agony, the medics come for the still unconscious fella in the back as others come to aid in the unpacking of food, vices and necessities, a female medic notices my limp even though I am trying to walk as normal as possible.

'You, OK, you need aid?' she says tentatively.

'Ah no thanks,' I say surprised as I look down.

'You sure? You're limping and are covered in blood,' she responds.

'Yeah, twisted my ankle, don't hurt much and the blood is from the dead plus from the guy with the leg wound,' I try to say as convincingly as possible.

'You sure?' she asks gesturing a hand towards me.

'Yeah, am good, thanks.'

I lie.

'OK, well if it gets worse, let me know,' she says with a smile as she then walks away.

I smile; if only there were more people like her in the new world.

I slowly limp off to my dorm.

I open up the door. Turning the handle felt like I had just shattered every bone in my wrist and hand.

I call out in a weak frail voice.

'K-Kim… Kim, are you home?'

No response; she is probably with her friend, I know she's in good hands, I take this private time to prepare and clean myself up, I turn on the makeshift boiler to prepare the hot shower water, I then slowly, agonisingly undress, I check my wounds, the ironic thing is that the superficial bite marks; if it had not been for the infection it would have undoubtedly healed within a week or two, the worst of the bites are the ones on my left thigh and right shoulder, the other two are just tooth grazers; even now after 6 hours after being bitten, they still bleed but it's not healthy blood, its black and lumpy and it smells.

I bathe myself under the warm water; still I have to stifle whimpers of pain as it feels the force of the water is stripping my skin from me, melting it away, it is only now that I fully understand the gravity of my mortality and it's like boulders on my shoulders that gain weight with each moment, I slip to my knees as tears begin to stream down my face uncontrollably, I weep not because I am going to die, but because I am going to leave behind alone the most precious thing to me, if there is an afterlife, if by some miracle, my spirit will linger, I will spend it watching over her, subtly aiding her, that is the only solace I gather in this time of despair. I gently wash off all the dried blood and dirt all the time wincing and whimpering, I can't take the pain any longer, with each minute it intensifies, I want to drip dry but know it would take too long, so I grit and bare it, to which again I brave the pain to getting dressed, not more than a second I place on my top without warning I vomit blood, the pressure of it drops me to my knees, I am sure both my patella's fracture and have broken my ribs due to the retching, I close my eyes and think of my daughter, I think of the days when she was born, her earliest birthdays, her first day of school, it works as the pain subsides momentarily, I feel the happiness, at the smile of my baby girl as she beams towards me, as she races her dog through the wheat field, her mother and I hand in hand as we gaze in awe at our perfect creation, I remember my wife, and what she told me the day she died.

'You look after our baby,' she said. 'You take care of her, make sure she is safe.'

She said this as the light slipped from her eyes.

I see my wife as she was; how I miss her, the loss I felt, feel, tears once again begin to stream from my eyes.

I inhale trying to compose myself, I need to be strong for Kim, I wipe away my tears and try to stand, I try but the pain is becoming unbearable, I think about numbing myself but I rebel against it I need to be fully aware.

So I sit in the dark remembering in agony.

30 minutes pass before I hear the door open, my heart begins to pound with excitement or terror, I try to stand using all my remaining strength, I am only capable of kneeling, I hear her voice call my name, I smile and I try to stand again managing to get one foot underneath me, I want to be vertical before she sees me.

'DAD!' she cries out seeing me doubled over, she rushes over trying to help me up but recoils when she feels how cold I am.

'Dad you're so cold are you...' she pauses her voice full of concern and worry.

'Am sick,' I say as I wince.

'What's wrong? What do you need... shall I get the doctor?' she says as she starts for the door.

'NO! No... I errr... just help me onto the sofa please,' I ask.

She hesitantly walks over to me and helps me onto the sofa, I hold back, the pain clenching my teeth.

I sit motionless and exhale through the pain, I look over to my daughter, her eyes are wide and full of confusion, worry and pain, seeing her beautiful face like that, the exact emotions etched onto her face when her mother passed, it begins to eat away at me, I want to hold her to tell her everything is OK, that I am OK, but I can't lie to her.

'Dad?'

Her voice breaks a little.

'I am... I was bitten,' I say looking down at the floor.

I feel ashamed I have let her down.

Silence. I force myself to look at her, I wish I hadn't, she seems petrified, frozen; the only thing that moves are the tears that stream down her cheeks, I can't hold back, I begin to tear up as well, I want to speak but I can't find my voice instead my mouth just hangs open.

'You can't...' she says as her tears fall faster.

'You can't leave me alone... you can't, I won't let you!'

She screams as she barrels into me wrapping her arms around me, the physical pain is nothing compared to the monumental heart ache that thunders in my chest, she cries openly and loudly, I failingly hold back my tears, I place my head on top of hers and close my eyes holding her, I begin to hope that this is just a dream and I am going to wake up soon but it's not and I don't.

I hold my daughter for the last time.

'I want to you to know,' I say in between sobs, 'that I love you with every fibre of my being and I always will as does Mum,' I say as I place her head in my hands and I look into her beautiful hazel brown eyes, she begins to cry harder.

'I… I am so sorry.'

I cry as I hug her again, she balls up her fists in my shirt and uses all her strength to hold me as tightly as she can.

My breathing is heavy and painful; I have begun to wheeze, time is ending, I feel weak, I can feel my heart beat weakening, slowing, she loosens her grip, the pain rushes in stinging, I try to ignore it but she can see it; I see it on her face, I know what I must now do, I have to leave my baby girl alone, the emotional turmoil that I face is unfathomable like a black hole that has opened up in my chest, sucked out my heart and now a raw angry wound sits aching, stinging, festering the skin sutured over it; the acid like infection seeping with rusted barbed wire, I lower my head as my eyes fill up.

'Dad,' she says her voice low and trembling.

I force myself to look at her into her eyes, I hate to see the pain so clearly in those eyes, pain that I have caused and pain that I cannot heal, pain that will stay with her for the rest of her days, I hate myself, I should never have volunteered to go out.

I know now that damnation exists, for only a damned soul could leave an innocent angel behind in constant pain to extinguish the light.

'Am sorry but you have to go now, honey.'

I force out this horrid sentence.

'What? NO!'

She protests again her eyes fill up.

'We can get the doc.'

'He can't help… you know that.'

I cut her off; even now she is hopeful, just like her mother; full of hope, but there is none for me.

Again, she begins to cry, I grab hold of her tightly.

'It will be OK, I promise, Zack will look after you now, he will take my place as your protector, guardian, he's a much better hunter than your old man anyway,' I smirk as I say but she continues to cry in my arms.

'Please, honey, you have to go now… I don't want… you know what I have to do.'

I begin to remove her arms from around me and push her away; this makes me sick as tears begin to fall uncontrollably.

'You have to go.'

My voice breaks as I unholster my revolver.

She sees the shiny metal gleam and once again she rushes to me wrapping herself tightly around me, I smile as I could never get tired of her embraces and for a slight second I feel peace that is broken as a new sensation spreads in my chest, a pain unlike any other one that I have never felt before but very distinct, its exact, brutal and sharp, it's a warning that the end is near.

'Kim,' I say her name, she looks up at me.

'Forgive me.'

I plead as tears once again fill my eyes.

She buries her head in my chest, I close my eyes and raise my head to the ceiling, I exhale then lower my head. That is all the answer that I need.

'You have to go now, baby girl, go.'

She begins to unfold from around me and steps back.

'I love you.'

The image of her is blurred as once again my eyes fill, she steps back one foot at a time, further until she reaches the door, I hear the handle turn and she says with a broken voice.

'I love you, Dad.'

Then the door shuts and she is gone, it's now; I break down, I can't control it, it flows wave after wave unending, again I look to the ceiling as I say, 'I am sorry.'

I say this to her mother, who I hope that she too will forgive me.

I cough violently, it feels as though my lungs are on fire, full of acid that is melting them away, as I open my eyes I see a crimson spray, now that she is gone and my focus slips back onto my condition, the pain barrels into main focus with every heartbeat; it's as though I am being electrocuted.

I thumb back the hammer, the metal clicks the firing, fine poised as the cylinder revolves placing the round in the barrel, I close my eyes and all I see is blackness, I feel dread as I pour into it, my arm moves and I feel the cold metal against my temple, my finger curls around the trigger adding light pressure, I focus on my wife and daughter, on their beautifully perfect faces, I focus on their smile, how they are holding each other, they begin to move each holding up a hand and begin waving to me, they smile as they do, and I feel love; I smile, my finger squeezes the trigger hard, I hear the dry metal click.

Pathogen

'8 hours in… another 4 to go,' I say to myself as I raise my head skyward or ceiling ward and begin rubbing my eyes with my thumb and index finger, day 6 out of 13 to which at the end I can look forward to a single day off where I will do nothing but catch up on glorious sleep, I try to focus my now distorted vision but find it painful to do so as the light seems to be horrendously intense.

I look down to my matte black shoes as my blurry vision fazes out and focuses.

A sharp, loud piercing sound echoes around the room, I hear the dreaded beep beep of the monotonal chorus, I exhale exasperatedly as my little reprieve is swept from underneath me in an instant, I push aside my crisp white lab coat to reveal the source of my annoyance, a little black pager that's hooked to the right side of my hip upon my leather belt and in tandem with the beeping noise it's flashing three codes.

3D1 – a casualty arriving unconscious or in arrest.

3D6 – attack or multiple attack.

3B2 – serious haemorrhage.

The last code is my specialty, I specialise in the area of haematology and pathology and this patient is said to have lost a large amount of blood but before I set off I notice the coding number three, that's the code for animal attack.

'Great, he's probably been mauled by someone's dog.'

I narrate to myself; it unsettles me. I picture in my head a rather large canine with bright red eyes, a mixture of rabid foam and human blood smeared all over its snout, I feel a shudder slowly crawl up my spine, I begin strolling down the hall towards A&E north wing, twisting and winding through the white corridors not stopping until I come to my destination.

I see the lobby in the centre is a circular desk that can be accessed from three points by either receptionist, doctor or patient. I see the night receptionist; she is talking to an older gentlemen.

As I approach the older gent, he realises my presence and ushers me forward then goes back to his clipboard, I quicken my pace.

Dr James Hersh is the head practitioner with 40 odd years under his belt; we all look to him for his wisdom and experience, the years however show on him, for the lines of joy and grief are etched into his skin, greying hair and beard, but everything about the man is pristine and immaculate; he was military. He doesn't speak of his time nor the experiences but we all know he was not just by his records of course, but also by the way he carries himself proud, strong and assertive, I stand waiting patiently 3 feet from him as he examines his notes, I am about to ask the receptionist a question when Dr Hersh finishes; he forcefully places the clipboard down and takes a few moments, I can see the frustration in his face.

He starts by exhaling exuberantly while clearing his throat and then slightly shakes his head. I can see it pains him, the loss of life.

'Five in total, three DOA and one critical, he's in theatre at the moment, torn jugular, they're currently pumping O positive into him, if they succeed am placing him under your care... I'd like him to receive his actual type,' he says tentatively.

I nod my agreement as always.

'Did they catch the animal?' I ask.

'Animal?' he responds incredulously.

'It was no animal; it was a man.'

My eyes widen and my mouth becomes a fly trap; the same shiver crawls up my spine, I begin imagining the feral man huddled over his recent kill while ripping off mouthfuls of raw flesh, eyes burning with true hatred, I pull myself out of the delusion and ponder my colleague's words.

'James, you mentioned five patients,' I ask.

'Ah, yes,' he responds, 'the officer first on scene is also a patient; he's currently being treated, he was bitten multiple times. Protocol dictates that he needs full blood work, in cases such as this, so I need a full report on that plus full blood work on the assailant, police suspect possible rabies but they need confirmation in order to proceed with CDC protocol... you already have samples from the assailant, a J Fowler awaiting in your lab, however, the responding officer, Officer Mills is currently in quarantine, the attending nurse will be bringing you samples to be analysed.'

I nod and smile.

'OK,' he responds as he then moves on to his objectives.

I continue past the main desk and as I do I see the fair face of the receptionist Evie.

She beams a warm smile at me and I return one in kind.

She is a lovely girl with gentle features, illuminating emerald eyes and pert inviting lips, what's fascinating is that her bottom lip is slightly larger than her top which gives her a subtle natural pout.

Anyway, I focus on my pending tasks and make my way to my laboratory.

After about 5 minutes of walking I realise just how fatigued I am; I look to my watch; three and a half hours left. I climb a flight of stairs; I prefer to use them as I don't like elevators... getting into a metal box dangling at great heights while putting your entire faith and safety in a steel cable. Nope. I push open the double doors from the stairs and walk into a hall way. In front of me is a sign, in big black bold letters that says, "Haematology". I smile and walk on through the waiting room as I do; in my left peripheral I notice something that catches my full attention, a vending machine but its what's inside it that; I notice the last cold gleaming can of relentless I must have it, I place in the correct amount of change and wait with failing patience, it arrives; I grasp hold of the immensely cold can, it's the shorter 250ml but I don't care, I am going to enjoy this, the metal lip clicks and hisses as I pull the tab back and take a full mouthful; instantly memories of my youth play in unsynchronised rhythms, I feel the energy and invigoration of the stimulating liquid.

I proceed into the lab with my cold can. I see the glass vials of red fluid waiting by my desk with the name J. Fowler perfectly written in elegant calligraphy, I know exactly who that writing belongs too.

I smile and walk over. Not long after I have sat down, the door opens as the attending nurse walks in with more vials of blood from the police officer.

I greet her with a smile as she replies in kind.

She places the vials into their individual holder in the rack, I notice the way she places them all facing me uniformly with standard printed labels all placed perfectly.

'Thank you,' I say as I look up into her eyes.

She smiles back and am sure she blushes a little.

She then strolls over to the cabinet marked blood vials, opens it and carefully retrieves a handful; I watch as she then leaves and notices as she glances back with a smile which confirms my suspicion about her blushing the first time as her cheeks are now more noticeably red.

I grin as I think and narrate to myself.

'Oh, what would your wife say?'

I take another swig of the energy drink and proceed on with my work.

I set up the microscope by flicking on the power, it hums to life and the glow of the LED illumination dock awakens, I ready my slides placing two glass ones to my right and a further two next to them; accidents do tend to happen although not too occasionally, I prepare myself by placing on the relevant PPE (personal protection equipment). I am not fond of the latex free gloves, they tend to make my hands sweat but nevertheless protocol must be adhered too, I place one of the glass slides on to the pick-up tray, they have finger holes at either side, a useful invention. I ever so tried to pick up a thin piece of glass off a table nightmare, I then take one of the blood-filled vials, I start with the police officer, it seems prudent a man of the law, I too place that into a holding station that holds the vial upright allowing both my hands free.

I begin by placing the first glass slide onto the illumination doc and then turning on the U2LED digital display; it's a LCD tablet camera that is android based and allows me to record everything through the microscope lens which are built in, everything that is recorded is stored onto a micro-SD card.

I open the first scarlet filled vial and then take hold of the automated pipette. I place the tip into the liquid and push the auto fill button with my thumb, the fluid shoots up into the clear plastic turning from a clear white to a dark red and then placing a small droplet of the liquid onto the glass slide, to which then I place the glass slide under the lens on top of the illumination dock but before I tune the eyepieces, I take one last mouthful of the energy drink and then place my eyes onto the rubber rests.

What I see at first is a blurry red haze, I begin tuning the optic lenses, a few seconds of blurry red haze and then perfect clarity. I see everything; red blood cells, plasmatic fluid, white blood cells, platelets, everything you would expect to see until I look up to the top right corner and I notice something unusual something that's not supposed to be there. It looks like a bacteria but it has immune system traits and not only that, it's firing; it has electrical signals, nerve endings, I raise my head from the scope and ponder.

'No… can't be,' I unnervingly whisper.

I check again and it's still there.

My hand moves on its own muscle memory, my index finger and thumb take hold of the rotation wheel and I adjust the lenses directly on top of the mystery, it's there in full view, I increase magnification slightly, now I see familiarity in the bacteria, it's defiantly a bacteria very similar to pneumococcal meningitis but it has other traits, its able to blend in with white blood cells; they aren't responding or seeing the bacteria as a foreign body but what is most confusing is the electrical firing. I don't know of any bacterial organism to do this, again I raise my head and puzzle this conundrum, I then look to the LCD camera, it's there but then something else catches my eyes again and as I look to see the same nerve firing it's more of the bacteria, a lot more and it's multiplying rapidly. I mean unworldly fast, I begin to breath sharply, this can't be, I remove the slide and quickly fill another auto pipette with the attacker's blood, then place a drop onto a new glass slide, the blood is darker, thicker, the slide goes straight under the lenses and my eyes to the rubber eyepieces. I adjust the lenses and magnification; the black ooze becomes instantly clear. I see the simultaneous flashing, the liquid is full of the bacteria, it's flashing at a monumental rate faster than the first sample and multiplying just as fast; the scary thing is while everything in the blood is dead these things are alive and moving. I look up to the screen again, I can't take it in quick enough; everything about this is not possible. I suddenly feel cold and not alone I spin to look behind me as quick as humanly possible fearing a horrible presence to see nothing. A cold shiver slowly crawls up my spine as my hairs begin to stand on end, this is not good, I race to the phone and speed dial Dr Hershel; he answers the phone and I tell him I need to proceed with the lumbar puncture on both the officer and the assailant, he begins to question me then stops.

'OK but I need to know on what grounds,' he says authoritatively.

'Unknown bacterium type of pneumococcal strain, CDC quarantine may have to be implemented.'

Silence.

'I understand; does it confirm the bacterium? I am on my way to you now,' he says sternly.

'OK,' I say nervously.

I begin gathering the necessary equipment in order to conduct the lumbar puncture.

After gathering my equipment, I await on Dr Hershand; as I do, my mind swims with horrors of cannibalistic feeding frenzies; people screaming and wailing while being devoured alive by glowing red eyed demons.

I am brought out of my nightmare as Dr Hersh bursts through the door. I am nervous, I nearly hit the ceiling, Dr Hersh looks at me with confusion.

I gesture him to the monitor attached atop of the microscope, he observes the dark mass and then turns to me.

'We need to get to the morgue.'

I hear his voice quiver.

We take off with haste almost sprinting down the corridors.

No words are spoken as we assemble around the morgue table, a pristine white laboratory cloth is draped over the corpse, Dr Hersh walks around the table directly opposite me and pulls at the cloth, I can barely contain my horror as I look upon this mangled being; the skin is as white as the cloth, dark veins spiderweb from what looks like bite wounds; chunks of flesh missing riddled with bullet holes and a single hole to the forehead. I begin donning the PPE (Personal Protective Equipment) as does the doctor. He sighs heavily then begins to speak; he clears his throat first.

'Let's get this over with quickly.'

He outstretches his arms and takes hold of the deceased's left arm, rolling him onto his side, I begin by placing the hollow needle at the base of the spine and slowly press it into the flesh directly into the spinal canal, I pull back on the plunger to remove cerebrospinal fluid; usually the fluid is thick, clear and colourless but the fluid that fills up into the syringe is a dull pink.

I look to see the worried expression on Dr Hersh's face.

We then proceed over to the laboratory microscope again. I make the necessary preparations and place a drop of the fluid onto the glass slide and place it under the lenses, I look through the lenses to see the same sight as I did with the officers sample, however, the bacterium isn't firing as quickly and seems to be dying, the other concerning thing is the amount of the bacterium cells within the spinal fluid, I estimate the amount to be ten times that of the blood sample taken.

I begin explaining my theory to Dr Hersh as I step back and as he looks into the microscope; he confirms my theory that the bacterium dies off when the host dies.

'We need to draw a secondary sample from the officer immediately.'

The intent in his words is almost hostile.

We race to the quarantine ward, as we arrive I notice the horrendous state that Officer Mills is in; he has a cold sweat but a high temperature, his skin is pale and sunken around the eyes, he is barely conscious. I state who I am and what procedure I am going to perform but no response. I look to Dr Hersh for advice; he shakes his head and insists that I follow on with the procedure, I gather my equipment as the doctor preps the officer, I draw my sample of cerebrospinal fluid, it's exactly like before, dull pink, I hastily pace over to another microscope exactly the same as the one in my lab, place in the slide with the fluid, adjust the lenses and the magnification to the perfect setting; what I see is impossible, I turn on the LCD tablet monitor to reveal my findings to Dr Hersh. I hear him gasp; we both can't fathom the words to voice a response at what we are looking at. The foreign bacterium is again massively abundant and firing, but at such a rate that it seems as though the bacterium is illuminated; the other thing that we notice is that any other cells that the bacterium comes into contact with it kills out right and with such effect its killing the host.

The silence of fixation is disturbed as the heart monitor's alarm sounds; the officer has gone into cardiac arrest, myself and Dr Hersh spring to action. I begin with compressions as Dr Hersh intubates the officer as a nurse bursts through the door and begins aiding the doctor, she takes over the intubation as Dr Hersh administers adrenaline and sternly requests the defibrillator machine.

He charges the machine as we stand back, the electrical charge passes through into the officer.

Nothing, he charges again and again but still no rhythm after almost 10 minutes he finally calls time of death.

'Death of Officer Mills at 03:45 a.m.'

You can hear the sorrow in his voice.

'Notify next of kin,' he asks the nurse. She strolls over to a white phone hung on the wall, she will contact the receptionist for his next of kin's contact details, after a few moments she strolls back over and aids us in removing all the equipment from the officer, a few minutes afterward myself, the doctor and the nurse take a few moments of composure; it's always hard, the loss of life; that's why we do what we do, that's why we are health care professionals, we help people, it's as simple as that and every loss is felt.

I feel someone take a hold of my wrist; I assume it's the nurse. I note that her hand is cold and clammy, I open my eyes as I hear the scream, it's the nurse; my eyes lock onto both her hands that cover her face, her eyes are wide. I look down instantly to see the hand of the officer wrapped around my wrist and his grip is tight, I then look into the eyes of the deceased officer as he looks into mine, I note the dull iris and vein riddled cornea; his mouth drops open as he lurches forward up off the bed.

'HOLY SHIT!!!'

This is my verbal response, the nurse screams again as I pull on my arm, he lurches forward; again, I react on instinct. It looks as though he's going to bite me. I hold his head back with my free arm, I look to Dr Hersh who is frozen with shock, I scream his name, I see him move forward. With exacting swiftness he takes a hold of the officer and pulls him back, the nurse continues to scream, we both struggle with the living corpse, it releases me of its own accord. As it does, Dr Hersh throws it almost across the room, it lands with a thud, a heaped mess; I see it twitch as it slowly lumbers to its feet, it can't be, he was dead and yet his body is moving.

'Officer Mills... Officer Mills, are you there, can you hear me?' the doctor exclaims frantically.

But no response, the corpse continues to amble towards us.

'OFFICER STOP!!!' I exclaim.

But no effect; it continues towards us.

It turns its focus onto the nurse, it lunges forward grabbing hold of her apron. Dr Hersh moves in to intercept the man but the nurse in her panic grabs hold of Dr Hersh placing him directly in front of her and the walking corpse; he tries to steady himself but the nurse won't let him go, the creature sinks its teeth into Dr Hersh's collar, they both scream as do I, the nurse lets go and backs off as Hersh begins hitting the creature in the face in an effort to release himself, it does not; instead, it clamps down harder on his collar, his scream is louder, I move forward, as I do, it releases the doctor but it takes a mouthful of his flesh, blood begins pouring down the doctor's lab coat. I move forward as it then sinks its teeth back into the neck of the doctor, his eyes widen as he screams, the blood begins pouring down his neck as it rips through the doctor's jugular.

Dr Hersh falls to the floor, I rush forward and smash my clipboard over the dead man's head, it stumbles back as it composes itself again, it lunges for me, my instinct is to protect myself so I raise my hands, it takes hold of the same arm as before but this time it takes a chunk from my forearm, the pain is excruciating and instantly I see the nurse run to me, she pushes it back with incredible force, it falls to the floor and as I fall to my knees, the blood runs, it streams and flows all over, I see the nurse kick the corpse back to the floor. As it begins to rise, once again, she then pushes it back to the floor by the defibrillator, she charges the machine, it begins to rise again, so with my last strength I throw myself forward and pin it to the ground, she grabs the paddles as the machine beeps stating its fully charged.

'MOVE!!!' she screams at me.

As I let it go and slide myself back she slams the paddles down onto the creature's head; the surge of electrical charge sears, burns and chars the corpses head, the smell of melting skin and burning flesh, it lasts only moments as the charge dissipates and the nurse removes the paddles, it lays motionless on the floor and the nurse readies herself for it to rise once again but it doesn't. I move over to Dr Hersh who to my horror has passed from blood loss, the nurse rushes over to me with multiple bandages and begins bandaging my forearm, I hadn't noticed until now but the phone is ringing, I ask her to answer it and ask her to get security and notify the receptionist to implement quarantine procedures immediately, she does as requested; at a moment's notice, she returns applying pressure onto my arm.

'Evie has already sent the security team to theatre, the other victim started attacking the surgeons while they were in the middle of operating on him, and she contacted the CDC and implemented quarantine procedures, no one in or out of the hospital,' the nurse says with glistening eyes.

'It will be OK,' I say but I am not convinced by my own words.

I sit staring at the lifeless corpse of my mentor feeling the pain in my forearm; the burning sensation that is slowly creeping its way up my arm, I close my eyes as a sense of dread takes over.

I look to my arm and notice the darkening veins beginning to spiderweb out from under the bandage.

I don't know what's going on or what's going to happen but this sensation inside my chest fills me with utmost sickening fear, that's when I notice the slight twitches of movement muscles spasms then actual finger movement.

Dr Hersh raises his head, I look into his eyes, the familiar dull iris and vein riddled corneas, he shambles to his feet and then I hear the scream.

Forever

The unfathomable emotion that is love overpowers the senses and distorts the mind, it empowers us to perform the impossible.

She laughs... I made her laugh... I adore her voice, recently, well, more like the past couple years, I've been looking at her in different ways seeing her anew and I like it, I like everything about her, we have been inseparable since our first encounter, we know everything there is to know about each other, friends closer than sisters but recently I have been harbouring new emotions that I have never felt before, strong powerful feelings I want to tell her but I am afraid of what will become if I do, as what I have to say will change everything, it's scary, I don't want to lose her and just the sheer thought of being alone without her, the horrid feeling that follows is almost indescribable.

I focus on a taxi that rests to the left of me, the black metallic paint that once shined so bright, dulled by the years, small holes pepper pot the entire side of the vehicle, all tires flattened, windows broken, I grimace as a rotting forearm hangs out of the driver's side, I hasten my pace as I don't want to see the rest of the mangled corpse, we have been following this meandering river of black tar and wrecked vehicles scavenging from the abundant abandoned cars, trucks, buses and other forms of vehicles, most of them are empty, I'll never get used to the sight of a dead body, let alone one that is up right and walking that hungers for living people, I may never get another peaceful night's sleep again.

Evie notices my ill content which she proceeds to nudge me with her hips, the momentum sends me careening into an abandoned car, I laugh and she smiles as her distraction has worked, I rest on the same car as I take out my water bottle and take a few sips. I then hand it to Evie, she takes it with a smile, she doesn't notice that as she took the plastic container she brushed my fingers with hers but I noticed I felt her skin touch mine, the spot where her finger tips gently rested. I instantly get a tornado of butterflies in my stomach as my heart seems to do backflips, I watch with awe as this angelic beauty quenches her thirst, I am not sure how long I was staring, it could have been a lifetime for all I know but I couldn't look away, for she is enchanting, she notices, she makes eye contact and smiles, I have to look away to find a way to stop the blood from flushing into my face, I look to the floor at my feet, I notice the encrusted mud all over my boots, the cracks in the tarmac, I can feel her looking at me staring inquisitively, why? Does she know? Has she figured it out? Did my staring too long give away my secret? I begin to panic a little, I want to look at her but I can't. I am frozen, I don't know how to react or what to do or how to be, why is it so hard to be myself, so I look at everything but her, the horizon how the sky and the land seem to crash into each other, the blue and the green colliding and how hot the sun is, I feel it on my skin, how it tingles, I feel the sweat roll down my neck, the heat coupled with the unnerving awkwardness of my present state of mind, the hot blood now pulsating around my cheeks. I look out to the endless green and notice how the grass sways towards us. I await with glee for the cooling breeze, the entwined scent of grass and subtle hint of wild flowers, but instead it's so sickeningly warm and the smell I had inhaled deeply hoping to get a cooling, respite from the heat but my reaction is the exact opposite, I begin retching, coughing and sputtering, the air is thick with liquifying meat. I immediately throw my hand over my face and lean forward as I feel the thick warm fluid rise in my throat, the stink is so overpowering, I feel as though it's consuming me.

After a few moments I compose myself seeing Evie recovering too but as I look to her for comfort, her prominent expression screams out with fear, I slowly turn my head focusing in the direction in which she is fixated, my gaze rests upon a black shambling mass that ebbs closer, it's a horde of those dead freaks ambling towards us, a moving wall of decomposing corpses, we stare awestruck at how it came to be that the recently departed could rise back up and ravenously eat the living as I ponder their existence, how they came to be, watching with such terrifying curiosity as they amble closer and closer; it suddenly dawns on me that they are heading straight for us and the sudden realisation that we are now in danger, I spin about facing away from the nightmare hoping to awaken soon but I don't, this is reality. I feel Evie's hand wrap around my forearm, she pulls me in the opposite direction of the undead, I hurl forward at such a pace. I feel as though I am flying in an instant. We stop and Evie pushes me to the floor, the concrete is hot and rough.

'We are cut off by another horde coming down, these are closer we need to let them pass,' she says to me while gesturing to roll under the car.

I do quickly roll to the far side to which she then drops and rolls next to me, both panting so hard, we try to calm the fire in our lungs, we begin taking long deep breaths, I notice the gleam of sharpened metal Evie holds; she readies her knife, I look to her, she seems calm ready to take them all on, her independence makes her all the more attractive, with shaking hands I slowly un-sheath mine.

We both freeze as we hear the rasping moans and shuffling and the unbearable stench as the danger ebbs closer. I feel the fear it ignites and it begins burning through my chest, my heart rate increases, I begin trembling. I stare up at the underside of the car, my mind races, the constant moaning makes it hard for me to concentrate in order to build a mental blockade against the fear but it's so intense it bursts through, my eyes move away from the cylinder shapes and wiring and I look right slowly turning my head. I see the different shades of grey and pale white flesh mixed with pink issues and deep reds of dried and fresh streams of blood. I force my eyes shut and turn my head back under the car, I once again try to focus, I think about the only thing that could take my mind off of the impending doom that lurches no more than 2 feet from me, Evie, I concentrate solely on her, her perfection, her emerald eyes, I focus on a memory the day that I fell for her, it was autumn; it was dark and we were huddled around the fire, she sat directly opposite me, she was laughing, we all were but everything around me is muffled and distorted, only she is beautifully preserved in perfect detail, I remember every aspect of her. She wore a red flannel shirt that gently hugged her frame, the sleeves rolled up to the elbows entwined in the wood smoke. I smell her perfume, wild berries, her hair emulates the glow of the fire and her eyes seem more illuminated, I become fixated on them and as the ashes slowly soared into the night sky she glances at me and flashes a smile, our eyes meet and at that exact moment my heart stopped, I began to tremble and the butterflies flurried and fluttered, I swim in the memory and for a moment I am calm but then she slowly changes, her beautiful frame becomes thin and skeletal, her white skin becomes a horrid shade of grey, her flowing red slightly curled hair transforms into a lifeless mass tangled broken, her face gaunt with dried skin stretched over prominent cheek bones, plump bright lips now mangled and torn showing stained teeth; the light freckles that dotted her cheeks and the bridge of her nose have now disappeared but most traumatic are her eyes, sunken and dark, the bright vibrant emerald green, her beautiful fierce gaze is now a dark dull hollow see through stare which terrifies me to the core, it's the most horrifying thing I could imagine. The image is branded into my conscience and from it a heartache to which is monumentally heightened that infects every single piece of me, it's hard trying to contain the anguish, my body stiffens and my hands grasp the concrete, my toes curl, my resolve is immediately compromised, the pain leaks out in the form of tears, they flow down the side of my face. I want to erupt, to scream but all I can do is stifle whimpers as the emotions fester and build and build, it's too much; death has to be better than this.

The tears continue to flow fast covering the side of my face but then they stop as a new sensation barrels through me, my left hand, its warm and soothing, I look through blurry eyes to see perfect fingers lightly touching mine, the warmth from them is sensational, I am mesmerised as they move slightly curling around my little and ring fingers, the grasp is slight but firm; I feel an electric surge, it's amazing, it sparks into me then fires up my forearm. I begin tracing the form of the fingers and the hand with my eyes drinking in everything, I proceed up the forearm. I can't help but notice as I trace the upper arm her pert breast. I watch as she breathes so calmly. I continue up the shoulder. her flawless pale skin is so inviting. I want to reach over and feel it on my lips, I trace her neck then the perfect line of her jaw. I realise that her head rested towards mine, I immediately stop on her lips, so beautifully full; they are emphasised greater by her pale skin, the lower is slightly larger than the upper but still just as amazing, I find myself and continue up until I meet her gaze, her beautifully exuberant emerald green gaze; she stares directly into my eyes, my mind blanks becoming fuzzy. I find it hard to think of anything but her and how my affections for this girl don't seem humanly possible, we continue gazing at each other not blinking not moving, I recognise her gaze, it's the look of adoration, happiness and love, my heart beats faster as the realisation sinks in; it begins thumping as though it's trying to break out of my chest and the emotion that follows is incredible. It goes throughout my body increasing in potency, the perfect antidote to my ill-content and anxiety, and the butterflies are whirling around as I realise her feelings for me, she smiles as tears begin to form in her eyes and her grip on my fingers tighten, reinforcing my realisation and then the impossible becomes reality, she mouths the words with those perfect lips.

'I love you.'

I mimic her tears and all, we lay under our car in our perfect little world, I want to hold her, to kiss her, I want to tell her I love her, I want her to hear those words, I want to hear those words from her, I am so perfectly happy, words cannot describe how amazing I feel right now and I now I understand that while I was stealing glances of her she was glancing back, I know now that the whole world has changed but we shall remain together through everything as we have

42

been doing since we first met; she is my forever and always will be.

Survival

The Cyalume eerily illuminates the immediate surroundings with a ghostly blue hue, I can see all of 7 feet around me, then nothing but blackness, it's as though the world doesn't exist, swallowed in to a singularity, with each footstep more objects materialise, the forms of each item become more apparent as the blue light slowly melts away the black, a wheel chair appears to my left, I slowly edge around it, trying to be as silent as possible but the uneasiness of the darkness knowing that anything could be lurking within it ensures that my heart rate is considerably elevated and my breathing fast, the corridor is long and full of unknowns, step by step I proceed deeper into the abyss.

My right foot comes down on top of something hard, stepping back, I bring the blue light down and what it reveals shouldn't scare me so but it does, a corpse lays before me it will never become a normal sight for me, they should be under the ground perished of natural causes, not like this, dried leather like skin, dehydrated, I notice that its limbs are missing all of them, I try to focus my attention from it to ease my mind, but as I hug the corridor wall, more and more bodies appear, it increases my already elevated heart rate, I try to calm myself but my mind races, I slump to the floor my breathing starting to hitch, the panic becoming more constant, the pain in my chest, the anxiety coupled with the burning in my shoulder and abdomen is almost overbearing, that is until I hear the rasping noises and shuffling in the distance. I immediately shoot to my feet and thrust my pistol out in front of me, my finger curled around the trigger, directly ahead my eyes scan every inch of the abyss fearfully anticipating for the shambling form to emerge with the lust for flesh in its dulled hollow eyes. I stand in the deafening silence, waiting for nothing, but nothing appears, my heart rate slows so does my breathing, I look at my pistol and slap it against my temple.

'Shit, shit, shit,' I frustratingly whisper attempting to knock my senses back to focus with the hard cold steel, then I holster it, no silencer, means noise, means waking the dead.

I knew that this would be difficult, but I need to treat my wounds, I need medicine.

'Fucking bastards,' I whisper recalling the reason for my injuries, bringing me to this place, at least I know they can't follow me.

I exhale and proceed forward, for what seems like an eternity. I slowly come to the end of the corridor, well what seems like the end is actually a corner, I hug the wall place the light behind my back and pear round, the darkness seems to brighten and I can see that it opens up, I proceed forward wearily, again step by step, listening for anything, I was right it is lighter and it opens up to a court yard, or main hall, I can't really tell. Cowering, I leave the relative known safety of the corridor and walk out into the open, it is the main hallway, the main entrance is directly in front of me, barricaded from the inside, I seem to be on the first floor, I am able to make this out because of the natural low light of the night, as my eyes adjust, as well as some of the building's electrical lights seem to be operational, the place has some lingering power, the wing to my right is lit up, and I now hear gentle pattering of water hitting glass, I look up through the glass roof; it's raining, I have always enjoyed the sound of the rain, and the sound it makes on the giant glass dome is soothing, I hear thunder in the distance, suddenly I am aware of being cold and wet but located on my left hip, my bandage is leaking, I need to hurry, grabbing hold of the metal railing I lean over to increase my eye line, my main focus is to look for the A&E department, antibiotics, bandages, pain killers, sutures and a safe place to remove the bullet, the thunder grows louder then lightening cracks and momentarily illuminates the hall. In that moment of illumination I see them, leaning over I see the small horde, at least 80 they stand in the main hall waiting, almost huddled together in the dark, some seem to patients or used to be as they are wearing the operational gowns, my wide eyes drink in the horrid sight before me and then they are all shrouded once again, but that image is burned into my conscience, every single muscle in my body tenses, I hold my breath, slowly, very slowly I move backwards until I hit the wall, again I shut my eyes as I feel the burning in my chest, I inhale a shaking breath, listen to the rain hitting the glass, the soothing sound, it helps, I open my eyes and raise the light, as I turn right I notice a picture on the wall, it's a site map, and it's telling me that the wing with power is the A&E department, but it's on the ground floor, the wing above is firstly a waiting room to which branches to paediatric, neonatal and perinatal wards, it states that there is a fire exit staircase that runs from ground to parking basement all the way up to the roof.

'OK,' I whisper shakily, and then I move down right to the corridor wall, as I step into the light I stash away my Cyalume.

I walk step by step, the corridors are almost pristine, I arrive at the main waiting room, I now have to go through the paediatric, neonatal and perinatal wards to get to the staircase, the waiting room is in little disrepair, some of the lights flicker on and in the right corner the ceiling tiles have fallen, the steel benches have been removed and placed atop each other to barricade the doors to the main stairwell, I proceed right through the doors marked paediatrics; this ward is almost immaculate, the lights are constant, and have a yellow hue to them, I assume to make it more like natural light, I move silently down the corridor, strange how the air seems thicker, stale in this area, I can see lots of dust particles hanging in the atmosphere, to my left is a glass room, I glance inside, all the neatly arranged baby beds in perfect rows, most with name tags still attached and the infants still wrapped within their blankets, all mummified looking, I guess this is where the proud fathers could look in and marvel at their newly born miracle, I notice a few adult bodies huddled on the floor holding their infants, seems as though they all starved to death, my eyes flick down to the glinting of light, a few syringes and glass bottles of empty morphine that contest my theory, I try to focus my fractured mind but this is evidence that society has irreversibly died and we are now nothing but wolves at each other's doors, I proceed on, after walking through the last two corridors seeing the small incubation chambers and even smaller life support machines, my mind becomes numb, finally I make it to the stairwell, its dark, the doors close behind me and the light fades, the air is cleaner and a horrid weight is lifted from my chest, I fumble in my pack for the Cyalume, the darkness once again melts away with an eerie blue hue. I proceed down into the abyss, minding my footing, the pain in my shoulder and stomach is noticeably more intense.

After two flights of stairs the sign stating ground floor A&E becomes apparent as the lights are still on like a beacon, it beams through the cracked door, I move to it, and listen for a moment, nothing but the deafening silence is heard, I move to the stair railing and peer down into the black, even though I can't see anything, I get the feeling that something is looking back at me, the dreaded sensation tears through my entire core, but I do not blink, I stare into it, then slowly I back away to the doors until my backpack makes contact, using my right shoulder I put my body weight and lean into it, the door opens and I peer through the crack, stood directly in my way facing away from me stands hunched one of the dead, missing its right arm and is donned in hospital scrubs, a doctor, I presume, once a life saver now a damned life taker, once again I stash away the Cyalume, my hand fumbles for the handle of my hatchet as I maintain focus, there is only one, maintaining my low profile, silently I open the door wider and squeeze through; readying myself, I lift my hatchet high, then with as much force as I can I bring it down into the top of its skull, the creature smells of dried blood, clothing almost immaculate apart from the blood stains and other bodily fluids, it's skull offers little resistance, my hatchet becomes embedded within its head, the creature's full weight falls into me, I let out a light gaffer attempting to hold its hefty weight, it exacerbates my wounds, the weight coupled with the pain, it feels as though my veins are about to burst, I attempt to place the former human on to the floor, I would like to say with no sound, but if any of the dead was within earshot they would have come running by now, I await for a couple seconds motionless, teeth gritted, lips apart and anxiety scribbled all over my face, thankfully nothing, I attempt to remove my stuck weapon with a single hand. It doesn't budge, I attempt a couple more tugs, nothing, letting out a frustrated sigh, I wrap both hands around handle then my feet onto the dead Dr's shoulders, I prep myself. Using my legs I press the body down, while I pull at the hatchet, both my wounds scream at me for such exertion, and I feel the bandage on my shoulder begin to seep, it starts off warm then becomes cold, I give it one last push, and the hatchet finally flies up into the air, as do I, almost landing on my ass, I look around to see if that commotion alerted any, a few anxiety filled seconds and silence, so I proceed forward and left, towards the main A&E ward, it's a massive expanse of space like an open court, the only thing that divides it are the dividing privacy curtains for each of the removable beds, I search all the trollies and cabinets, it's a gold mine. I find everything, sutures, forceps, swabbing alcohol, iodine, pretty much everything, that I need apart from the antibiotics, am not surprised it's a cache horde, as this hospital was an FOB (Forward Operating Base) for the military as they poorly attempted to control the outbreak, I stash the supplies into the front pocket of my pack zipping it up, and continue the hunt for the antibiotics, if it wasn't for the bullet still imbedded within the meat of my left side I think I could have done without the antibiotics, but I can't help but thank that they never deemed it prudent to practice their aim, a little to the right would have been a gut shot, my intestines would have been shredded by the impact and energy, as for my shoulder a little higher than the bone would have splintered probably severing the artery. I bleed out, or a little to the right again and my ribs and lung, drowning in my own blood, I grit my teeth and focus on the task at hand, as it is, I would have been able to just swab the area with the iodine then suture them both up as best I can, but because I have to go "digging" I need them to stave off infection, I get lucky, I come across a door marked pharmaceuticals, I try the handle, its stiff and doesn't move much, locked.

'No door is ever locked.'

I reference from a movie, as I pick it open.

The lock tumbler clicks reassuringly, and the door swings open, I can't believe it, it's practically full, antibiotics, pain killers, actual morphine, as well other pills and medicine I can't pronounce, even chemo bags. I exhale a huge sigh of relief, I grab as much broad spectrum antibiotics I can and morphine and then head to find a secure place to conduct my surgery; as I leave a stack of white handled items catches my attention, the red script reads "medical skin stapler" my eyes widen and I grab three of them.

I retrace my steps back to the staircase and proceed upwards.

I find a nice office on the third floor, it has lovely skylight, the rain continues to patter on the glass, I found as many lamps I could as the power is still on in this part of the building possibly due to the back-up generators, that or the power to the city hasn't yet gone completely out, either way I am thankful, this office has secure privacy blinds and the door can be locked from the inside without a key, and the sofa looks really inviting, soft fabric rather than cold leather, I also managed to scavenge a couple cans of Dr Pepper, a Mars bar and a bag of tortilla chips from a vending machine that I had to pry open, I was hoping that the sandwiches were still in date but of course nope, but what I have is a lovely luxury that I will enjoy… after.

I pace with my heavy legs to the large sofa, remove my pack and then the bandana covering most of my face, with difficulty I remove my jacket, shirt and vest, the movement agitates my shoulder wound which burns and bleeds, I remove the dark red bandage and add a white one, instantly the centre begins to turn a dark scarlet red, still holding the bandage in place, I move to the desk and sit in the chair, it's just as comfortable with lumber support, that soothes my weary muscles, I remove the files as well as desk objects from the desk then place on the lamps and mirror. I lay out my surgical equipment, drop my trouser to my ankles then sit back in the chair, I look at the hole in my side, the things we have to resort to for survival now, humans killing each other for nothing more than the items in their pockets, packs on their backs, the worst parts of the so called human condition have truly been set free, and with each day brings new atrocities that I must witness, with each one burned into my memory my sanity breaks just that little bit more, we used to believe that we were the superior beings of this planet due to our ability to reason, its only because of our so called higher brain function that we believed we are above the animals, but once our society collapses anarchy ensues, and we will literally eat each other, I shake my head, I remember the men's faces as they died by my hand, I am a killer too, but the only difference is I don't enjoy it, I do it only to survive.

I listen to the rain, it helps strengthen my resolve, that it was either me or them, and my guilt wanes, then the burning pain grabs my attention.

I am in two minds about which wound to treat first, I decide my shoulder as its hardest, I look into the mirror, the bullet went through and through, I have an entry and exit wound, easy to manage, I swab the areas with iodine, which was a bad mistake, as I forgot to numb the area first, it's like I just dropped acid onto the wound, I continue as I started, swabbing both areas then injecting antibiotics into both areas, then use the skin stapler, the front side was easy the back not so much, I had to use butterfly stitched to hold the skin together while I then gently placed the stapler in position, pressed down then pressed the activation lever, the sharp pain, is instant but fleeting after moments it's the constant throbbing pain that is annoying, which is a lot easier than suturing the bastard, it's all finished with bandages that are taped down, now I work on the worst one, this I know I can't numb cause I have to feel for when the forceps have it, I try to rev myself up but I know this is going to suck, once again I swab the area, and once again the acid like pain boils all around and within the wound, I grit my teeth and try to overcome the pain, it doesn't work, moments after the pain slowly subsides, I then swab the forceps with the sterilising alcohol, placing my left index finger and thumb at either side of the wound then very slowly stretch it open, my jaw clenches tight, as I place the forceps just above, the realisation hits me hard, as what's about to happen, I look away and around as my eyes begin to tear up, I wipe them and try to focus, I need to focus, I need to get it done, again I place the forceps over the wound, I exhale, then hold my breath and tense my core; my toes curl, as the forceps dive into the wound, initially I don't feel anything, then as they go deeper, a hot stinging sensation begins. I continue holding my breath and tense as hard as my muscles will allow and then some, using the forceps, all I feel is tender soft flesh, that is until the tip of it hits something hard, that's it! I place both ends over the foreign object within my body then clamp down on it hard ensuring that I do not lose grip, once I know I have a firm hold I remove it quickly, the pain is instant sharp then blood flows. I place the forceps with the bullet down on the desk then begin to stem the blood flow; it pools its warmth as it runs down my side, the pain throbs, I finally inhale as my body screams for oxygen, I am sweating profusely, the adrenaline starts to flee, the blood stems due to the bandages stopping it, gently I swob and wipe up the excess blood, I am shaking, I inject liquid antibiotic into several places around and within the wound, then staple it up, swab then bandage, I sit back in the chair feeling the intense burn in my abdomen and waning throb in my shoulder, I focus on the rain pattering on the glass above me, again the thunder booms in the distance, my vision becomes faded, my breathing shallow, I pass out.

I awake several hours later, the pain in both areas has veritably gone, only a dull ache remains which is a monumental relief, my eyes find the copper projectile and I look at with disdain, I dress myself with some extra clothes from my pack and then open the tortilla chips; the salty crisps are a nice change and the mars bar is bliss, but I wasn't expecting the shock of the soft drink, the taste takes me back, memories of family and friends, poignant moments in time, happy moments, I find myself tearing up, becoming lost in the memories, I enjoy the happiness they bring, I sit and enjoy my reprieve.

Not an hour after I lay on the soft sofa and sleep, my plan is to wait till morning, evaluate my situation, maybe scavenge for extra items then leave, and continue with my survival north and with any luck find my partner, we got separated due to the ambush, I hope he is OK, we have been apart almost 48 hours now, and I miss him terribly, I want him to find me, to come through the door like a hero, to say my name and then hold me tightly in his arms, I force back the tears, for now I will lay and dream.

I am gently awoken by the rays of light from the sun warming my face through the sky light, I sit up, muscle memory takes over and I check my pistol, removing the mag, confirming its full thumbing in the safety, finally slightly pulling back the slide to reveal the single round positioned within the breach, I then change my bandages and take some oral antibiotics with another can of Dr Pepper, I dress, place on my pack, I go back to the ground floor with a second bag and fill it with extra medical tools, equipment, medicine, anything and everything that will help us get to the mountains and then for after.

As I meander around the hospital I become complacent and my fear fades, big mistake, fear keeps you on edge, keeps you sharp, stops you from fucking up, and that's what I do, I fuck up, I stride round the corner into a new part of the hospital on the third floor, right into a bunch of the dead, I stand frozen, instantly fears fingers grip me, she is never far from me, she holds me intently in her icy embrace, I can almost hear her whispering in my ear. I begin to slowly walk back as my hand moves on its own to my pistol, I notice one that catches my attention, a young girl, early 20s probably, she has multiple bullet wounds pepper potted about her body and face, the right side of her is also burnt and her stomach seems to have been excavated, as what's left of her intestines hang down from the gaping hole, she has jet black hair, to her shoulders, I know her, and as I remember her, her head slowly turns and her eyes lock on to mine, without hesitation, she immediately starts shambling towards me, the dead look in her eyes is washed over, and replaced with a violent desire to tear in to me to slake her unending hunger, I realise it's time to leave, I make for the fire exit back the way I came adjacent from my office camp, I am not sure why I am running as they can't catch me, fear or survival response I guess, I reach the exit door, pushing the grey steel lock bar, it swings open and I feel the cold spring air gently caress my face, the sky is blue and cloudless, the sun bright and warm, the fire door shuts behind me, as I bound down the metal stairs something catches my eye that stops me in my tracks a massive mass, at first I am unsure then as I focus on it, the shapes of bodies become more apparent, the entire main parking lot is covered in bodies, the mass thickens towards the underground bay, a mass grave site, hundreds upon hundreds of bodies piled upon each other, some lay within matte black body bags with the yellow bio-hazard symbol covering the centre, others in make shift body bags wrapped in painted polythene, or blankets stained red, most just dumped as they were, I suddenly see movement, a horde of the dead come ambling up from with the underground, like demons ascending from the depths, they move slowly into the heart of it and begin feasting, the self-destructive nature of the human condition taken over materialised within the remnants of the dead, I stand terrified, I can't go back inside and the risen dead are blocking my exit, I don't know what to do.

Dead

Bleak and desolate, a harrowing landscape, skeletal frames of dead trees loom off in the distance, the sun captured behind menacing clouds casting a dark shadow upon the land, a baron wilderness decrepit and decaying, there is nothing left of the world but the ghosts of the past haunting the survivors of mans near extinction.

Nothing natural survives in such a place.

I have wondered the earth surviving since the evil dead won the ancient battle of supremacy for the earth, their triumph over God. I have seen things that would crumble the sanest of minds… I have done things that people in times past would have condemned my flesh and prayed my soul would burn, but in these times of madness the actions I commit and scenes I witness have become a normality.

Scenes such as the reanimated corpses of the dead feasting ravenously on the living.

The living murdering the living for the shoes on their feet and scraps in their pockets.

And in more severe scenarios people eating people.

And so in the land of the dead killing has become a modern chore.

A daily chore.

I keep to the shadows.

I remain in the tree line, my silhouette is camouflaged amongst the deformed trees ensuring my safety, but all senses are kept on constant alert remaining ever vigilant.

The surviving souls are often wolves in sheep's clothing, these times of severe desperation brings forth the true nature of man, the nature of hostility, malicious intent and violation and these damned souls torment, maim and victimise the weaker beings those who are not willing to perform such acts of barbarism, they pummel, plunder and murder without cause mostly for entertainment.

For those who value life they scramble to keep a hold of their humanity to not become corrupt by the darkness creeping in their hearts, the constant dwindling population take solace in the past, sharing stories of family, friends, dear loved ones, keeping their souls alive with hope of a world's future redemption… dreaming… hoping.

This is for those who cannot cope in the reformed hell, it is a momentary escape.

I do not part take in the murdering of the innocent or the momentary escapes as each will serve you up on the silver platter for the reaper, and I have no intent on becoming anyone's meal.

I would like to say that I am free of all emotions, it's true; I don't feel joy, remorse, empathy or guilt amongst others but one that is constant, that is unending… the rage, it's hard to suppress and over the years it has manifested into a creature that in my weakest of times takes over and I become the monster.

Smoke! Southeast… I smell it before I see it, probably a settlement, a rundown shambling shanty town brimming with disease crippled beings that were once people, desperately clinging to some scrap of semblance of what life was once like before the nightmares tore free from the imagination and now linger in the shadows.

Venturing over from a distance, conducting a full recce (reconnaissance) of the area and the inhabitants deeming them friendly or hostile.

The smoke becomes more dense as I approach.

Thick wood smoke fills my nostrils, I can now see the embers soaring effortlessly in the hot air glowing brighter against the coming darkness, I tentatively place my right leg down moving cautiously forward.

Instantly I freeze.

Immediately the sense of danger has risen dramatically, my right hand moves with its own mind to the handle of the blade strapped to the left side of my chest, grasping it with white knuckles, the reason for my ill content, intwined in the smoke a scent of burning meat, a scent unlike any other but as distinct as roses… human flesh.

My eyes scan everything in full, after a moment I deem safe and continue forward, but I keep an eye to the floor for trips (trip wires); if they are cannibals they will have hidden snares, snares with horrible intent not to kill but to maim, moving forward slowly no sound, my heart beat is slow, only the wind is whipping through the creaking branches, eyes and ears perked ready, my hand still tightly grasping the blade's handle, the smoke grows thicker and so does the stench, I kneel in the tree line of a clearing, I see a small settlement with four cabins all ablaze, three others destroyed.

No sign of life, no movement apart from the fire hungrily waving in the wind as it devours the wooden homes.

The people that inhabited these dwellings are all dead, I have come to witness the aftermath, I move in from the tree line; there could be items I could scavenge but looking at the state of the place my hopes are not high.

Continuing to move with caution calmly assessing, I realise that the actions that took place in order for the blaze to occur was no accident, the evidence is clear so far; a body hangs in the trees, a male riddled with bullet wounds, blood slowly seeping from them, I see that there are several bodies hung. All are male, all with the same wounds, pepper potted with holes covering the torsos. I stand and stare perplexed for the way they are placed, the positioning it has purpose, they can be seen from all angles of approach, all apart from the north towards the hills shrouded in darkness.

This was thought up by murderous minds, minds that want to send a message to any others who come this way, a message of fear.

In the centre of the settlement in between the blazing homes is a monstrous pile of the remaining inhabitants, brightly burning as I near, the flames come alive, they seem to flick out and roar in my direction, the flame has a taste for flesh, the limbs of the poor people are all contoured and twisted, ceased in their last horrible moments of pain, they were alive as they burnt.

As the flames begin to weaken, I move closer, and as I do I see a small hand reaching out to the sky through the mass of charred smouldering bodies, too small to be adult.

A child, tiny frail fingers, an innocent, and there are more, children not yet seasoned enough to know the depravities of the devil and his minions, children too young that they are not capable to survive on their own will, I lower my head as my eyes close.

I often hear as I wander from place to place from those peaceful enough to allow my presence, they speak of how their god has a plan that he lets Lucifer upon them to weed out the true believers and their reward will be salvation to be allowed in to his palace, they speak of God and his plan and his love and his forgiveness.

I dare to think that I could be forgiven but then I see the world around me, how it is now, rotting from the outside in the despicable acts being committed throughout the lands and I realise the truth that God left this place a long time ago.

I gleefully surrender to the creeping darkness.

A darkness that rages… that hungers with a lust to spill oceans of blood.

The darkness creeps out from my core worming into every vein, artery, capillary, into every cell, into my very fibres. I feel it with such heightened elation, it forms a monster with a hunger, a hunger that I aim to slake.

My eyes open with intent, the fire illuminates more evidence as it flickers, twists and contorts; it reflects off of a small shiny object that lays silently at my feet, a single shell casing 5.56mm, it belongs to a weapon probably an AR (Assault Rifle). I will need to be cautious, however, I will make it so they never see me until I snatch the life right out of them. The fire also illuminates more spore, the tracks are definitive and easy to see, sloppy but then again their arrogance is reason enough to allow this slack, the tracks lead all around throughout the camp heading off to the north to the shrouded hills.

And so I begin my walk into the dark.

I have been meandering my way through this land without purpose since all I knew ended and now to have a purpose once again, the walking seems to be taking a lifetime, I want to quicken my pace, the monster wills it so, but I know from training and experience that to rush could lead to disaster, and I am but a man so I walk savouring the coming blood sport, it's strange that I am anxious to kill; it is all I can think of. I swim and dive in the deep thought pools of death, for what seems days has only been hours, the anticipation intensifies as a scent flows through the trees.

Once again smoke, I am so close, the beating in my chest quickens and I feel the sudden surge of adrenaline, I should prepare, I stray off to the left deeper into the trees finding a large enough tree with appropriate flat group, it will provide some shelter, before I rest, I put my back to the trunk as I take off my pack and un-shoulder my rifle gently leaning it against the hard bark to prepare camp, I will wait until the night is darkest, when my prey will be slumbering; this irritates me for my impatience hastily grows, so I busy myself. I gather tinder and kindling and using my flint and striker start a small fire not too large to give away my position but enough to keep me warm, cook my food, sanitise my water, I empty my pack of all the necessities of war and make them ready, I place a crow that I caught earlier onto the ashes then take out a coke bottle filled with untreated water which I pour it into two canteen cups filling them to the brim then placing them too on the ashes.

I take off my coat and unclip my shoulder holster with my favourite blade attached at the chest, I pull out my Colt M1911 pistol, it's steady 2.44lb weight holds firmly in my right hand, the high beaver tail grip ensures for a tight precise shot, the beautiful firearm holds an 8 round magazine of 9mm Automatic colt pistol ammunition with one in the chamber, firstly I check the sights then begin to clean the weapon taking apart the braid blasted slides ensuring the hammer and trigger work correctly, I always ensure when I can that it is clean and works magnificently, once I am satisfied I take the two extra clips, remove the bullets one by one ensuring both clip springs work smoothly then thumb the ammunition back filling each, it is ready but as a last resort, bullets are precious commodities, I thumb in the safety then place it neatly back in its holster clipping it back around my shoulder, the next pistol I clean is my SIG Sauer P226; it is a lighter weapon, only 964 grams. It's a mechanically locked recoil operated system, it's not as powerful as the Colt but it does its job.

It's strapped to my right thigh again. I remove the side arm from its holster, it holds a 10 round 9mm parabellum clip. I grin as I recall the quotation, parabellum is derived from the Latin, si vis pacem, parabelum "if you seek peace prepare for war" and I intended on seeking some glorious war. I have an extra clip which I clean and ensure that it and the weapon both work amazingly. I place it back in its holster and thumb in the safety.

I then pick up my beautiful M24 sniping single fed bolt action system, this beautiful piece holds one chambered 7.62x51mm NATO A168-grain round ammunition, it comes with a five round internal magazine and is effective at 800 meters (875 yards); it has a magnificent 2,580 foot per second muzzle velocity and can render a man's head into several pieces, the typical action time is 4 seconds per round however I have a modest 3 second action time, this is only achievable by the stability of the bi-pod that allows me to focus all on the smooth action of the bolt, my breathing and target that my cross hairs rest upon, I visualise the pink mist and the high elation I get with each perfect shot, one shot, one kill. Glorious, the sight is a Leupold Ultra M3A 10x42mm fixed power sighting system, for this perfect piece of armament death. I have only 12 rounds left which I will save for a more dire time, I only wish I had more for it is a sin to keep such a beauty on hold.

Again I go over the entire weapon cleaning, inspecting making perfect.

The water has boiled clean, I let it cool then pour one of the two full canteen cups back into the plastic bottle, the last I add some pine needles and let it simmer some more, I pull off a piece of the crow, it's a dry and fibrous meat and taste like any other carrion bird.

Last but certainly not least I begin to ready my formidable friend, I wake my blade from its slumber, I hold it tightly, a Fairbairn-Sykes fighting knife with a blade length of 7 inches double edged, it becomes an extension of myself.

I sit preparing the blackened steel, listening to the grating of the blade over the stone knowing with each stroke that it becomes sharper, battle ready, each grind is a whin of thirst for the crimson liquid, I sit feeling the warmth of the flickering fire, the smell of the cooking bird, the pine needles the citrus sent they release, I take a sip and devour more meat, at this point I would sleep but it's not safe, it's never safe so instead I sit and listen to the rhythmic grind of the steel it's comforting.

Warmth emanating from the glowing fire, crackling of the kindling, the scent of fine wood smoke, the grinding of steel, bright embers floating carried up by the rising heat, a cool breeze, the subtle realisation of my surroundings, I awaken.

I look over my blade to discover that it's the sharpest it has ever been, scalpel like; the whole blade is matte black apart from the shiny gleam of the sharpened edges that smiles at me and I smile right back. The evil stirs within the strength that emanates and a powerful will to do violent and vicious obscenities that would curdle even the devil's blood and send him weeping to the safety of his burrow.

On this night I have decided I will release it, embrace it, harness it, make it my own, tonight I shall become the monster in the deep black that lusts for the reaper's embrace.

I slide my blade over the strop removing the burrs and increasing its potency, then sheath my friend and devour the last of the bird and sip down the hot citrusy water, I place all the items apart from those I will need for into my pack and stash it into the dark crook of the trunk while putting out the fire sweeping dirt onto it with my foot, and as the light fades so do I.

The night is hot, jet black, no moon shines far, she hides in fear, no stars gaze down, they have all gone elsewhere sickened by the brutality, the earth is cascaded under the reaper's cloak.

In the shrouded hills an actual piece of living hell has risen from the depths and now rests on the surface, the malice and evil of this hellish stronghold is enough to quiver the strongest of hearts and break the strongest of spirits.

A woman screams a cry of pain, the shriek echoes for miles then nothing but eerie silence, a horrifying realisation of the dreaded fate that awaits all.

Crimson thick fluid meanders down through the trees trickling over roots; it's source is an overflowing pool of blackened coagulating blood, the hole was once a grave with an initial purpose for a single unnamed poor soul but due to the sloth like nature of these defilers now a mound of bodies lay un-peacefully atop one another, decomposing skeletal frames of women are piled high it's evident that even demons seek the pleasurable flesh of women, the stench of rancid putrefaction hangs in the air.

This mass grave lays to the north east of an old logging facility protected by an 8 ft perimeter fence, just outside of this fence before the tree line, this is where the leftovers lay, all contoured and broken.

In the centre of their haven a huge fire blazes, illumination and warmth, the stench of human flesh thickly sits in the surrounding atmosphere, two buildings remain, the rest are nothing but broken corroding carcasses that the others have constructed into shanty shacks to keep off the cold elements this is the home for the band of hellions, approximately 13 strong with automatic weapons, that know how to be used.

Laughter! Two raggedly dressed villains come stumbling out of the secluded fortified gate carrying a fresh corpse for the pile, they walk out sniggering and joking, shuffling closer to the human heap ready to dump their deposit, one slips on the blood sodden earth, the other giggles then they heave the body onto the mound, she falls atop the others, the slap and clap of cold clammy dead skin contacting with decomposing remains is heard aloud; as the body rolls she comes to rest, almost stood for; the pile of dead hold her up, her bare skin is

61

pale against the diminishing light that reveals her beauty, that is if her lips were pink and not a shade of blue, her lifeless dilated black pupils stare into mine, jet black hair, chest length contrasts against her flawless pale skin apart from copious large black bruises that riddle her, the rivulets of fresh blood streaking down her limbs and the single 9mm hole in her forehead not exactly centre on but top right.

Such a waste of life.

The two fiendish creatures stand and admire their work, one making a vile gesture while placing his hand on her chest, rubbing, squeezing and remarking how she is still warm… he is the first, the second male laughs turning his back on his fellow fumbling with his zipper he urinates, he exhales exuberantly into the night air, head raised to the sky, eyes closed, he believes he is safe, a moment passes, he begins to piss on his own foot as the flow weakens, cursing he calls out noticing that his companion is unnaturally silent, he looks back to find the excruciatingly dreadful gaze petrified upon the face of his companion; terrified, he realises how his friend is stapled to a tree at least a foot from the ground, throat slashed blood water falling, belly gutted, the smell of fresh stomach acid and bile fills his nostrils, lumps of large and small intestine lay on the floor surrounding the nailed corpse; my second quarry stands completely fixated upon his brethren, breathing hitched in his lungs, panic taking hold, tears forming at the eyes, body quivering, all focus on the shockingly vicious and despairing sight set before him; he doesn't notice the monster in the shadows swiftly approaching. The fixated man senses the impending danger around him, his muscles tighten, freezing him, he now feels the exact same terrorising and debilitating fear that he himself has enforced on the innocent, a loud popping and tearing is heard as my victim's left knee is smashed. Out he drops in absolute agony but before he can sound that pain his face is pushed down with an unnatural strength, fully submerging in the stinking blackening thick red liquid, his head is held under until his lungs have flooded, he gargles and chokes, writhes and wretches then goes limp.

I rise from my second kill, I shake with intense adrenaline, I feel the cold thick liquid dripping from my hand, I exhale my fiery pleasure into the night, I am not sure why but I relished greatly in the killing of these foes and am now filled with glee far I know more are to come.

I move out slithering silently into the gloom hiding in the shadows.

Moving through the gate it opens easily. With a slight rusty squeal I fixate my eyes on any movement, on shapes that do not belong, to my half left approximately 30 meters one man sits by the fire slumped over in a dilapidated chair snoring away in a drunken stupor, even from this distance I can smell the fumes of whiskey, the whiskey bottle lays to his left, the delicious sour mash liquid still sits patiently inside, my spoils of war.

Directly in front, 40 meters, a shack like tent structure is riddled with holes and built upon remaining bricks.

Sobbing and whimpering to my right emanating from the largest building, it seems someone is still enjoying his spoils.

I also notice to the right 10 feet from the first shack another sits.

My agitation boils as my wall of patient's hastily breaks apart, I hunger to kill.

After slight meditation I decided on my third, which I assume is the leading devil.

I move right, my intention is to circle right and around through the compound taking out any who cross my path, like a wild fire I will obliterate all.

Soft feminine weeping coupled with male grunting, the stench of forced sexual contact worms its way into my nostrils, I ignore it.

The bastard is held up in the small building, a small fire from inside coupled with the main centred blaze illuminates the room and I see the animated shadows from the side window to the left door, gently and silently I enter the room, his back is too me, no clue of my presence too engrossed in his prize, he has the poor girl broken and bruised, face down on the rotten table, back arched, blood and tears covering the surface, another broken and battered body lays in the back left corner, she too is bare, already used, crumpled and unconscious. I would say she is dead if not for the wheezing and movement of her ribs, evidence of life.

I stand to the right behind the fucker savouring the kill; my muscles tense inching forward. I remark to myself this is too easy.

My grin widens then I strike.

With my left hand I grab his filthy face covering his mouth and wrench his head left; a popping crack is heard as my right hand plunges my knife into his exposed neck, I force it in all the way to the hilt then twist clockwise 180 degrees, bone and muscle try to resist with no use, not only have I severed his jugular vein and carotid artery but torn apart the brain stem and displaced vital vertebrae, arterial blood pulsates and sprays the walls, he twitches, I hold the lifeless body as the blood rains around.

The powerful influx of adrenaline courses, it's a massive high.

I can feel fear, smell it, the sheer overwhelming force, it's close; my eyes are drawn to the floor, there the tearful fear filled eyes meet mine, she lays huddled, blood splattered, black hair mattered and wildly tangled, she tries to cover herself with her limbs, I lay the corpse to the floor with no sound continuing eye contact, she begins to tremble, a lone tear falls from her dull brown eyes, I slowly remove my knife from the neck, the crunch of bone is easily heard, her eyes widen and she hunches up closer to the wall, she doesn't make a single sound and with my left hand I gesture for her to stay low, stay put then place my index finger on my lips for her silence.

A moment's pause and she acknowledges. I make my exit.

I move to the right of the cleared hovel still concealed, slowly moving to the edge peering round.

Half right about 30 feet I see them.

The next two are stood tormenting the remaining women that are in poor condition, some naked, some wearing torn and tattered rags, all are huddled together for warmth, they are in an office building but the front walls have been torn down and steel bars have been placed in line, it's a cage, they stand shouting vile obscenities pointing, spitting, deciding, having their fun, they all weep and huddle together, I need a distraction.

While I ponder, I overhear a name called and make a bold choice, I stand and move forward out of the gloom, my shape is recognisable and easily seen, I prepare my voice and I call the name.

'Hash.'

One turns and stares at my figure; I assume that's the owner, it's a gamble playing on their ignorance and arrogance but I enjoy it thoroughly, he stands inspecting.

'Over here,' I say as monotone as possible.

'Got a special one for ya.'

The swaying fiend smirks after taking in my faked voice and stumbles over to me.

'Have fun.'

The other remarks while turning back to the petrified prisoners.

Hash continues to walk towards me, he's giggling with excitement, I stifle a little giggle myself for I know he won't be giggling for long.

It's working; my gamble has paid off and with each foot step my glee heightens, closer and closer my anticipation peaks, 10-foot, 8-foot, 6 foot, I am shaking with eagerness, my patience grows thin, the anticipation is overcoming, he's mumbling talking probably to me but all I can focus on is stabbing his face numerously until there are no features, just a red blackening hole gushing brain and blood.

3 feet. He's close enough now to recognise that I am unrecognisable, he pauses.

His eyes widen as I grab him by the throat crushing his larynx disabling his speech, then drive my blade deep into his stomach, wrenching it upwards into his chest slicing and causing an open pneumothorax, this is also known as a sucking chest wound in which air moves from the atmosphere and into the chest cavity, it can lead to hypoxia, it is painful and if left untreated can lead to a very slow death, I drag him deeper into the shadows, we both disappear predator and prey.

I kneel over my quarry still crushing his throat, knife embedded, slowly I twist my blade left then right he feels it, footsteps, the other is approaching, he heard the scuffling, weapon drawn, a beretta M92 9mm, its shiny surface glints, I am low down in the gloom, he is unsure of my position and aiming in the wrong direction, I stay motionless, muscles ready, coiled viper-like waiting for him to enter my domain.

I wait for the perfect moment, he turns attention drawn, I move up directly in front of him, he focuses on my face inches in front of his, teeth-bared eyes wide almost glowing with murderous intent, the shock is sudden and instant, I silence him with effective speed by thrusting my blade deep into his chest, ribs cannot stop my rage, I pierce through the middle of his heart, I feel the beating vibrations through the blade, my knife giggles with the joy, I lower another corpse and remove my blade, the unparalleled pleasure that follows the kill is divine, it ripples through my core out wards to my fingertips, I feel it in my skin and veins, I love it. I wish that it doesn't end, it's strange that on this night every kill is enjoyable, I have never felt like this while taking another's life, it's surprisingly addictive.

I like it.

I pursue another fix.

Leaving the bodies moving past the cage of weeping women, still covered in the dark I now stand directly to the rear of the compound staring into the centred fire, the shape of the man still slumbering away in his chair, and the lovely bottle of whiskey that I haven't forgotten still wait, I now see the littered bones of their meal's femurs, ribs and various others strewn all around, to my right is the smallest of the shacks and next the other is situated; I look back over to the bottle, the light twinkles off of it, the left side of my mouth creeps up into a grin, my head turns to the nearest shack, the thing from inside wills me on, urges, pleads, begs me for its next fill and its cries do not go unheard and I move to my unaware prey.

Inside the shack it hums of body odour, alcohol, wood and cigarette smoke. I creep over to the far right, the man who snores drunkenly, peaceful for he believes that he is safe; such irony, he sleeps on his back. Gently, I place my hand onto his head and manoeuvre it turning his face away from me exposing the base of his skull. I place my blade millimetres away from his skin angled upwards aiming at the C1 cervical vertebrae, I tense my striking arm, muscles like coils I steady his head, add a little pressure then push my blade in, the sharp metal separates the C1 vertebrae from the skull base and the pointed tip stabs into the brain stem and spinal cord, he is killed outright, no pain, no fear, no sympathy, or requests of mercy, no pleading or weeping, I believe a death too kind for this bastard but I cannot wake them all, no matter how much I would like to pitch my newfound strength against them, I give all three this kindness.

I hear movement outside, getting closer silently, I move to the cover of the door, it swings open, the open door conceals me, he walks in oblivious to the dead men and myself, he moves in, in front of me and I move up.

Simultaneously I knee him in the back of his left thigh deadening the muscle while covering his mouth with my left hand; he falls back into me and I hold his weight, I yank his head to the left then shove my blade deep into his neck severing both carotid artery and jugular vein.

Pain he feels it but is unable to scream, my knife made sure of that; instead of screaming and whimpering he gargles and spews on his own blood, his trachea is severed and he's drowning in the very life fluid that his body needs to survive, he twitches and flinches strongly at first but as his own heart pumps out his life so does his strength, eventually he goes limp, lifeless, I drop another corpse to the floor, the room is now full of the smell of blood. A thick iron tinge looms in the atmosphere, I inhale it deeply appreciating my own work, my heart beats throbbing in my chest, sheer joy washes over I can barely contain it.

To my count four remain.

I walk out into the hot sticky night; the fire has taken most of the shadows I am in the open.

Voices from the front shack, the one solitary man by the fire still sits slumbering, voices grow more coherent rousing from slumber, I stand too, then move over to the side of the shack, the only place the fire cannot illuminate, hidden once again.

Two men walk out of the front shack, they begin to walk forward towards the main building probably to converse with their leader, I grin.

'What a sight they will see.'

I murmur and move forward silently behind them both.

I am close enough to hear their conversation speaking of how they should be given more rations and better picking of the women as they are the ones with the higher experience doing more of the work than the rest.

I have heard enough; I start with the left one, I grab his head, yank it back doubling him over and sink my blade deep into his chest, I must move quickly, I spin to my right, and am now face to face with the other, the first body drops to the floor lifeless with a thud, confusion and shock grips and contorts my next target's face only for seconds, my left fist connects with his throat. He gasps and throws a hand around his neck and begins to inhale rapidly and cough, he will recover from this that is if I allow him too.

I snatch his right hand with my left grabbing it by the thumb and twisting it outwards; the pain is instant as his wrist snaps. He throws a left fist in my direction, swiftly I duck to my right, he misses, exposing his left flank, I have to release the broken hand or expose myself, the dirty bastard. How dare he strike at me? I grasp the extended arm and bring my knee up hard into his stomach and again into his chest, then bring my knife down into the middle of his back, I manipulate him around so that he now stands directly back in front of me. I stun him with a massive head butt, he slumps to the floor and I sheath my blade, with both hands I hold his head up then violently twist it to the right while pushing the bottom jaw up breaking neck vertebras and the spinal cord, breaking C3 to

C5; this section of vertebrae are supposed to protect the part of the cord that controls the diaphragm, however I have just broken and dislodged them tearing the cord, his breathing stops and he will eventually die of asphyxiation. He flops to the floor, I wait as the life in his eyes ebbs, his pupils expand covering his iris, black, dead eyes gaze through mine, another two gone.

Moving into the front shack I notice it's partly built on brick; I have come for the remaining sleeper, he's nestled in the far-left corner, I move over to him; standing over, I stab repeatedly into his chest plunging my blade to the hilt multiple times, the rage erupts into a frenzy. I feel the ribs grinding and breaking with each stab, on occasion I have to saw my blade out of the chest cavity when it becomes lodged, warm thick blood oozes from within covering everything. I continue like this for a while until a hole has formed and I can see spine, rib, lung and heart in several pieces.

I look upon my work, my strength ebbs momentarily then returns with a renewed fury.

I am almost finished.

Steadily I walk out to the last man, my heart pounding in my chest, he still sits in the open slumbering away by the warmth of the fire, walking over, my monstrous shadow cascades over him, I watch him sleep with envy for I haven't slept like he is right now in a very long time… my anger bursts erupting pure seething hatred, I rip him up from his seat, he awakens as he flies forward landing head and shoulders into the fire he screams and scrambles to rise from the scorching flames but I rest my right boot upon his back and force him deeper into the glowing heat ,he writhes and screams as the flames consume his face, embers rise up into the night sky, the fire grows, hungrily it melts away the hair and skin, popping sounds emit as the eyes burst, his screaming becomes deformed more guttural and animalistic as the fire burns away the flesh from the inside of his throat, the smell of cooking human meat plumes out and flows over.

I hold the scum down in the blaze for an age, this is fitting, his soul born from the flames and will be taken back by them.

The writing and squirming has stopped, nothing now but burnt bone and meat. I take my foot off of the smouldering corpse, turn back, walk two paces forward and pick up the bottle of sour mash liquid, I put the cool glass opening to my lips then lift it skyward taking a few mouthfuls at once, then stop, the instant warming burn as the liquid flows down calming me, I inhale deeply then exhale.

As fast and sudden as the darkness took its hold, it's gone, my muscles feel like fire as though my blood has been replaced with acid, breathing heavily, waves of satisfaction crashing throughout, I stand for some time and relish. I feel the warmth of the fire on my back, my shadow is cast in front of me, I believe that it is my own, but as I look scrutinisingly it stands on ceremony, the fingers seem elongated and pointed and I see horns protruding from my head, I add another mouthful of the warm whiskey.

It's effect is amazing.

I glance back to see my shadow is my own again.

I take another the effect is greater so.

I go through the routines in my mind, I clean then sheath my blade, I check my Colt, a full clip and on safety the same for my Sig, not a single bullet used my grin widens further.

Screaming!

Instantly I realise what I've done or lack of what I should have done, I sprint down to see the reanimated body chomping at the women through the bars; in my extreme meditation of the slaughter I had forgotten the one rule, the one that should always be followed, the rule of ending the body completely, destroying the brain to ensure that the virus doesn't reanimate the corpse.

I stride up to the creature without fear, swipe it's legs with my right leg, it falls and before it can begin to rise I stomp it's head into a brain and bone pulp.

I continue throughout the compound completely cleansing it of the undead.

I move on to check the buildings, the two women now huddling together under the table flinch when they notice my presence and clutch each other tightly, I crouch beside them and gently place over them a blanket which I acquired from one of the bunks, they are submissive and weak, trembling, I help them to their feet and we walk out. I hand them clothing and turn as they dress.

It seems cruel but I lock them in with the others, I see betrayal etched on their faces, but it's not what they think, to be honest I don't care what they think, I cannot have them running amok taking things that I need, and possibly maybe turning their fear to anger, turn that anger to men, to me.

However, I am not totally deprived of all conscience. I hand them extra clothing and build them a fire closer for warmth, hand them food and hot drinks, then I busy myself going back to the main buildings searching the place, I find many things, the men were hoarders.

I proceed to rummage for supplies, seeking treasures.

I check all the places of concealment twice.

I go through the corpse's pockets for anything useful; mainly I find narcotics, blunt knives and other useless items, I do find something as I check the inside pocket of two victims, it's an old picture, ripped, torn, crinkled he stands with his arm around another man, the same that lays next to him both slain by my hand.

Brothers?

An instant image, a memory of preoccupation flashes in which I quickly cleanse.

I place back the photo and set to my routines.

I pile my victims high, douse them in accelerant, strike a match and throw the yellowy flame atop of them.

I take all 9mm ammunition and I acquire an M4 colt carbine as I go through cleaning and maintaining the weapon. I go over the specs in my mind thoroughly. 5.56x45mm NATO gas operated rotating bolt magazine fed selective fire shoulder weapon with telescopic stock, this hardy piece has the picatinny rail system. I attach a tac torch to the left side of the rail system, I scavenged four 30 round magazines and have filled all four with 5.56mm rounds with some to spare; before I load in the magazine I dry fire the weapon a few times ensuring that the rotating bolt actions properly and then switch the select fire options from single fire to three round burst to fully automatic finishing off by placing it on single fire. I extended the stock. The rifle is now 33inch in length with a perfect length of pull, I look down the iron sights ensuring they are accurate and not damaged, I will test it later with live rounds to see how zeroed it is, I flick on the tac torch to see it's working properly then flick it back off, I shoulder the weapon then attach the four magazines to each other. I unshoulder my new acquired assault rifle, pack a two clipped magazine into my thigh pocket then jam one clipped set into the rifle and set the safety on.

Again I scour the compound further seeking high and low.

After roughly three quarters of an hour I have thoroughly found all the hidden amenities and equipment I could find. I have placed the most of what I need into a pack and the rest I place in a pile in front of the women, all the amenities for survival plus luxury vices and weapons and ammunition, I stand ready to leave, I look at the prisoners and they sheepishly look away averting their eyes after making direct contact with mine.

I hold up a small shiny metal object in my right hand, the light of the fire dances off of it, I liberated it from the leader, the eyes of some of the women light up when they see it. I move forward and stare intently without blinking at each of them, most look down, but one holds her gaze, and I stare back, I note the fierce emerald illumination of her eyes, she shields another women behind her.

'None of you will follow me,' I growl intimidatingly.

She nods in agreement and I notice sincerity in her eyes.

I hold out the key and place it on the ground directly in front of her, I cannot risk contact, I leave the key on the soil and back away, she holds her gaze as do I; as I continue to back away, I see her take the key from the earth but she doesn't go for the door she waits continuing to stare at my figure as it blends into the blackness.

I return to my hidden belongings emptying the ones I acquired from the compound placing them into my own pack, then on my back, I smile as I reach for my rifle, she has waited patiently for me, I introduce my rifle to my new assault rifle as I sling the M24 over my shoulder, I take a few mouthfuls of water from my canteen, screw back on the lid then place it back on my hip, I ready myself, my blade left chest, colt under left arm safety on, sig strapped to right thigh safety on, M24 shouldered left safety on, M4 shouldered right safety now off.

I proceed into the darkness continuing my romp to nowhere.

The sun's presence is imminent, I mingle from tree to tree. I've been moving for three days straight.

I continue forward for some time.

I believe it to be midday, the sun beats down, all focus drained, my steps are weak and small, I am shambling, my eyes are heavy. I am incredibly fatigued, my muscles ache, legs like stone, I continue my walking unaware of my location or where I am headed, I never do, I just wonder, my head blanks, all I hear is the rocks and dried leaves crunching and crumpling under my feet, my breathing is heavy but surprisingly soothing concentrating on the sounds fixating on each breath.

In… out… in… out.

Calm as everything tides away, total peace, I feel nothing, no fatigue nor pain, happiness, love, nothing total and absolutely nothing, I have reset to my now normal state.

Subtle moaning and guttural grunting to my left along with shuffling feet, my head turns to the source.

Dried tanned hide barely covers animated bones, wisps of white hair fragilely cling to what skin remains on the skull, actual walking skeletal remains, they move shambling, shaking without a purpose as the brain decays and dehydrates, shrivelling; so does the electrical firing of the neurones they weaken and slow, they lose all focus and drive, they lose the hunger, becoming meandering hollow husks deprived of emotion, thought and purpose they are nothing, another appears to my right walking into focus then another to the side of that they all look alike, I am the odd one out in appearance, no character neither notices me, I hardly noticed them, we continue to walk side by side for a while longer, I ponder the reanimated beings, and notice a similarity, like them I am deprived of purpose, I meander through the land with no home, no place to belong, deprived of thought and emotion, dead as they are, I am nothing but a hollow husk of a human with a dark heart full of evil intent wandering the earth until my end comes, until then I keep walking as the undead do, keep moving forward, keep surviving, to continue my mundane and monotonous existence, this is how I live now.

This is my life in hell.

CPSIA information can be obtained
at www.ICGtesting.com
Printed in the USA
BVHW051307180423
662562BV0001 6BA/911